FIRE
IN THE
VALLEY

Center Point
Large Print

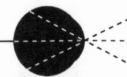

**This Large Print Book carries the
Seal of Approval of N.A.V.H.**

FIRE
IN THE
VALLEY

Steve
Frazee

CENTER POINT LARGE PRINT
THORNDIKE, MAINE

This Center Point Large Print edition is published
in the year 2014 by arrangement with
Golden West Literary Agency.

The text of this Large Print edition is unabridged.
In other aspects, this book may vary from the original edition.
Printed in the United States of America on permanent paper.
Set in 16-point Times New Roman type.

ISBN: 978-1-62899-322-6 (hardcover)
ISBN: 978-1-62899-323-3 (paperback)

Library of Congress Cataloging-in-Publication Data

Frazee, Steve, 1909–1992.
 Fire in the valley / Steve Frazee. — Center Point Large Print edition.
 pages ; cm
 Summary: "Bitter feud turns to bloodbath as Major Whitlock fights his
way through a range war"—Provided by publisher.
 ISBN 978-1-62899-322-6 (hardcover : alk. paper) —
 ISBN 978-1-62899-323-3 (pbk. : alk. paper)
 1. Large type books. I. Title.
 PS3556.R358F57 2014
 813'.54—dc23
                                                      2014028601

Chapter One

The icy needles of an evening rain were drilling into Major Whitlock's clothing as he unsaddled the smoke horse before the cabin in the valley of the Upper Arkansas. It was June 16, 1868.

With the honest tiredness of a long day's work lying pleasantly in his muscles, Major's thoughts were on kindling a fire and cooking supper. It was always good to be home.

He slapped the horse away and started inside.

It was then he saw the rider coming down the road from the north mesa. The man was riding without hurry through the wet gray pall. For a half minute Major stood tight and still, the heavy saddle in one hand, the bridle under his arm.

Then suddenly he broke away and went inside and put the gear away against the cluttered south wall of the cabin. Again, he stood motionless for several moments.

He was a square-faced, solemn-looking man, only shortly past his twenty-first birthday. His sister, Dorcas, had once yelled at him in anger, "You're just a pokey old grandpa, Major! That's all you'll ever be!"

And that was when he was sixteen; he was much older now than the five years difference.

No, he had not recognized the horse. A dark bay,

he thought, though it had been hard to tell color in the rain.

The loft ladder lay at his feet with a pile of harness, tools, oxen yokes, and other gear piled on top of it. He threw everything aside quickly and thrust the ladder up into the loft hole.

It was gloomy up there with the only light coming from spaces between the overlap of shakes. Near the fireplace chimney, the bed where Dorcas had slept was still neatly made, dusty. One of her worn-out dresses hung from a peg in a rafter.

Rain made a gentle pattering sound on the shakes while Major was rummaging in a wooden chest. Maybe I'm being an idiot, he thought. Dozens of strangers use that road. Just because I didn't recognize him or the horse is no reason to get nervous.

When he climbed down he was carrying a pistol, holstered, wrapped around by a hand-tooled belt.

He buckled it on and went outside.

The rider had stopped at the foot of the hill on the far side of the valley, sitting his horse in an easy go-to-hell manner, as if it were a sunny day. He looked up and down the valley and his whole attitude was a bold appraisal of the land.

In forty-acre plots that took in all the fertile bottomland and reached onto the mesas on both sides of the valley, was Whitlock land. The rider was not the first to cast greedy looks at Deer Valley, but no one before had been so openly contemptuous of Major's presence.

Still in no hurry, the rider came on. He swung west to avoid the black morass of the road and that was further insult. Major had spent many back-breaking hours hauling rocks to make the road passable so that travelers would stick to it instead of cutting his meadow to pieces in a dozen places.

With bleak distrust Major watched the stranger. A dark bay, sure enough, powerful, short-coupled. A double-cinched rig, strange to this country. Bulky in a woolen coat, the rider looked wider across the shoulders than Shad McAllister, and that was some big for any man.

His sodden black hat was down-tilted in front. About all Major could make of his face was a wild, black beard that gave him a rough, mean cast.

With black mud dropping from its pasterns, the bay came up the little rise from the meadow. Without slowing, the rider turned the horse directly toward Major.

"Just a minute there!" Major said.

Man and horse came on steadily. Major put his hand on the cold, wet butt grips of the pistol.

The rider stopped. The downward hunch of his neck and the hat brim still hid his features. "Danged if you ain't the spitting image of one of old Brant Hurlbut's blue tick hounds getting ready to jump into a fight."

7

"Lafait!" Major yelled.

Lafait Whitlock raised his head and tipped the hat back in place. White teeth flashed in the coal-black beard as he swung down to shake hands with his brother. "I wondered all the way across if I was going to get shot in the belly."

Except for heavy brow-structure, there was little resemblance between the two. Lafait's eyes were Indian-dark under black brows and his skin was swarthy. He took after the Whitlock side of the family, while Major, with sandy hair and complexion, looked like a Stuart, on the male side of Ma's family.

By the time he had finished cooking supper, Major had imparted about all the family news he could think of to give Lafait. Dorcas, married to Toby McAllister, had named their baby King. Young Jude Whitlock was with a survey crew somewhere in Middle Park. Ma and Goodwin were getting along just fine. She was doing most of the running of the store while Goodwin chased around on his other business deals.

"Goodwin laid out a townsite around the store," Major said. "He calls it Badger City."

Lafait grunted. "That'll ruin the country."

After supper Lafait sat on the raised fireplace hearth, his clothes steaming from the heat. Above him, festooned with soot streamers, were the deer horns he had set into the chimney. Pa's buffalo gun and the old Pennsylvania long rifle were racked there.

So far, Lafait hadn't volunteered one word about his year in Texas, so Major raised the subject.

"How'd you like it down in Texas?"

"All right, I guess."

"Miss the mountains?"

"Some." Lafait rose and took the long rifle off the deer horns. "Where's some rags and grease?"

While he was cleaning the weapon, Major tried a different approach. "Carl Burnine has got a lot of kin scattered around Texas. A couple of cousins visited with him a spell this summer."

Lafait's deep-set dark eyes flicked up and studied Major. "Don't beat around the bush."

"I won't. The cousins said you killed a man down there."

Lafait put the long rifle away and took down the buffalo gun. "Two men," he said bleakly.

First, the miner at Goodwin's store when Lafait was barely eighteen. Even the man's friends said it wasn't Lafait's fault, but still it had come about. Then Cy Grove and that other fellow.

Cy Grove had been bought and paid for. He'd killed Pa. It had been a general fight up there in the sandy gulch when Grove's bunch tried to get away with some Texas cattle. No one could blame Lafait for what he did. But now there were two more dead men.

"Jeem's cousin!" Major blurted. "You just can't go around shooting people, Lafait!"

"Don't figure on it."

"What happened in Texas?"

"Horse race. They got mad when they lost." Lafait sighted through the rifle barrel, holding the breach toward the fire.

"Is anyone after you?" Major asked.

"Nope."

It was time to get off the subject, Major figured. "You going to stay here now?"

"What for?"

"The land, man! We've got a place. Those ten calves Blake gave us are doing fine. I got five bred heifers from Burnine last fall and they all sprung good, healthy calves. Before long, I'm going to get a bull from him and—"

"Seems you and old Burnine are thicker than thieves, Major. When are you and Susan getting married up?"

Major frowned at the interruption. "The time isn't right. It's not because of Susan that Burnine's helped me. We're good friends. He gives me a lot of advice."

Lafait grinned. "So one day he says it's about time you and Susan ought to hunt up a preacher, and since you always take his good advice—"

"No, no, it's not like that, Lafait. Don't get off the subject. I'm trying to tell you that one quarter section of this place is filed in your name and a third of everything that's here is yours. We even got a brand, the LJM."

"That sounds good," Lafait said. "How about Jude, right in the middle of that brand—you think he's ever going to come back and settle here?"

Major got the coffee pot from the fireplace. He poured into the tin cups and handed one to Lafait, and then he sat down on the edge of the long table. "I don't know about Jude. He's different from you and me. He might not be back—for long."

"You know danged well he won't, but you keep bluffing folks away from here by saying it's his land and he'll be along directly."

"How do you know what I've been doing?"

"I stopped at Bill Gifford's this afternoon."

Major gave his brother a look of disgust. Gifford was a sore spot between them and always would be. He had been a friend of the man who killed Pa. Against Major's wishes, he had courted Dorcas, who thought he was wonderful, until she ran away to marry him on her seventeenth birthday. One night with him had changed her mind, and there had been no marriage.

The next day Jude and Major had found her walking in the snow, trying to run clean away from her family because she thought she was shamed forever. Jude took her home and Major went on to have a little talk with Gifford, telling him quite simply that he wouldn't live long if ever he spilled a word about the mistake Dorcas had made.

As Major saw it, the Whitlocks had a considerable score against Bill Gifford, but Lafait excused everything, saying that Gifford had nothing to do with Pa's death, which was the truth, and that Dorcas had a right to do as she pleased.

Lafait was an odd one when it came to sticking up for someone he liked, no matter what the person did. Here he was, coming home all the way from Texas after being gone a year, and he took time to stop a few miles from Deer Valley with a man whose place on Indian Creek was—or, anyway, had been—no more than a hideout for bushwhacking robbers.

"Still the old mother hen, huh?" Lafait said, grinning. "Don't fret yourself, Major, Bill ain't doing nothing but raising a few horses. No cow stealing, no stage robbing, no—"

"How do you know?"

"He told me."

"Jesus Christ!" Major said. He drank his coffee and scowled. "Forget Bill Gifford," he said. "Now let me finish telling you about the place here."

Lafait sat down on the hearth and stretched his legs. Steam vapor was still coming from his clothing. The rain was making a steady whisper on the shakes. "Shoot away."

Major told him all about his plans to develop Deer Valley. "The only reason we left Kentucky was to get a prime piece of land. Planting stuff, won't work here, so I don't even think about it no more. We got all the hay we need and good summer grass on the mountains, so the main problem now is getting enough cows."

Lafait leaned back against the chimney. He grunted something which Major took for approval. But after a few minutes, right in the middle of a sentence, Major said, "Damn it, are you awake?"

Lafait opened his eyes. "Your main problem ain't getting cows. It's trying to hang onto your land."

"Bill Gifford, huh? He must have told you plenty."

"I would have guessed it anyway. From the time you first seen me, you stood stiff-legged."

"I didn't know you," Major said. "You sat out there like a wolf staring at a sick calf. What was the idea?"

"I was glad to be back, that's what, so I was just looking. Then I realized you didn't know me, so I tugged my hat down and had a little fun." Lafait pulled at one of his boots. "Man! I think that growed to my foot."

He swung the leg around so the boot would get more heat from the flames. "You run inside and put on a pistol. I seen rain streaking through dust on the gunbelt."

"I haven't touched that pistol since a month or two after you gave it to me."

"Yeah," Lafait grunted. "So what's happened lately that made you run for it just because you seen someone you didn't know coming down the road?"

It was hard to explain. So far, it was all hints, sly remarks, indirect threats by newcomers who couldn't find good land to take up, and who said no man had a right to three claims.

Major hesitated. He didn't want to sound like a scared old woman, for nothing had happened so far.

Lafait put it bluntly. "Folks are sore because you're hogging this whole valley, ain't that it?"

"It's not hogging!"

"The hell it ain't. Why not admit it?" Lafait grinned at his brother's anger. "I say like you—keep it, but there's no use to try to act holy about it. Just do what you're going to do." Lafait raked a piece of wood close with his foot and tossed it on the fire. "Who's doing the heavy talking?"

"Since you left, there's a half dozen new families in the country, the Lavingtons at Kettle Drum Springs, the Stenhouses, Eben and Uriah Martin, the Groslands—and others. All of them have shot off their heads about some of us having too much land, and they say something is going to be done about it one of these days."

"What?" Lafait asked.

"Hell, I don't know. If I knew what they had in mind, it wouldn't be as bad as worrying about what they might do."

14

"Being all alone here with three claims, you do more fretting than, say, the Pilchers, who claim more ground in their end of the country than a man could find if he tried to measure it off."

Major walked over to the hearth and stared into Lafait's wild, beardy face. "I ain't begging you, or no one else, to stay here and help me hold what belong to the Whitlocks. You can go to hell if you figure I'm begging you, Lafait."

"It ain't the Whitlocks no longer, it's just you," Lafait said calmly.

"I don't understand you, Lafait. This is your land, as well as mine and Jude's. Otherwise, why'd we come out here? If you don't want your share, say so! And if Jude don't want his share either, that makes no difference. I'll still stay here, and I swear on Grandma Ripley's grave, somebody will have to kill me before I give up one inch of Deer Valley."

Lafait's gun muzzle eyes gleamed in the firelight. "I knew that long ago. You're the one that would've shot old Rusk dead that day we run 'em off, not me."

That was the truth. It had scared Major at the time. Any threat to Deer Valley always roused a fierceness in him that left him shaken afterward.

Lafait stood up and yawned. "When you get married, if you feel about your wife like you do this piece of ground, a man would be risking his life to say good morning to her."

"I ain't figuring on getting married very soon."

"Might sweeten your disposition some."

The fire was burning low and the rain had stopped when the brothers went to bed.

"Where at was it you had the trouble in Texas?" Major asked.

"Just a camp. There was an old fort called Phantom Hill not far away."

"The way you shoot, Lafait, it looks like you could wound a man—in the arm, say—instead—"

"Not if I'm getting shot at. All I can think to do is kill him."

When Major asked another question sometime later, Lafait was asleep.

Chapter Two

There were times just for looking, like this morning after the rain. Clean shaved, in his best clothes, with the horses saddled and waiting, Major stood outside while Lafait was still piddling around in the cabin. The world seemed brand new, all washed and aglitter with sparkling droplets on the meadow grass, and even the plunging gray slopes of the mountains looked friendly.

It would be a prime day.

"We going or not?" Major yelled.

"Just hold your horses a minute." Lafait came out shortly afterward, buckling his pistol belt.

"You don't need that to visit Ma and Dorcas."

Lafait hesitated, with the end of the belt in his fingers, ready to shove it back through the loops. Shaved and with his hair trimmed, he looked ten years younger than the man who had scared Major into putting on a pistol the day before, but he was no youngun; something in his eyes and the set of his mouth denied that. Yet, when he grinned suddenly, some of the boy he had been came back and the memory tugged at Major's heart.

It was hard to believe that Lafait had killed five men.

Turning back to the cabin, Lafait unbuckled the pistol belt as he walked.

They were mounted and ready to go when they saw the riders just breaking over the hill. A few moments later Major saw the wagon, with more riders behind it.

"Pilchers," Lafait said. "Is there a wedding or something?"

"No." Major got off his horse.

It looked like every Pilcher in the tribe was around the wagon. The old uneasiness returned to Major. Ross Pilcher and his three broods of offspring from three marriages were neighbors ten miles up the valley, having come to the country in the same wagon train with the Whitlocks. While there had never been any real trouble between the two families, they weren't what a person would call real friendly either.

Matt Pilcher and Major, the same age, had courted the same girl on the way west. They both lost.

Studying the riders carefully, Major observed that old Ross wasn't among them. For quite a spell now the father had been sort of shoved aside.

Lafait swung down and sat on the chopping block, trying to smooth wrinkles out of a pair of striped pants he had taken from his warsack the night before. Now and then he glanced out into the meadow, where the wagon was already having heavy going.

Matt was in charge, sure enough, and as usual, he made a big show of his authority. Major watched him ride up to the wagon, waving one arm, directing the driver to turn out of the road. Instead of trying any of the numerous rut marks beside the road, Matt forced the wagon clean over onto unmarked sod.

Major cursed under his breath. He'd talked a dozen times to the Pilchers about chopping up that meadow. The more ruts, the more water settled in them, and then the boggier the whole crossing became, and the farther to the side wagons would go to miss the mud. Major could foresee the time when about forty acres would be cut to ribbons.

"Rusks, by darn!" Lafait said.

"What?"

"Rusks. In the wagon."

They had to come closer before Major was sure. For a fact, it was part of the Rusk clan in the wagon. Lonzo was driving. The year before, Jude and Lafait and Major had run Lonzo's whole bunch off the lower meadow when they tried to settle there.

Matt ran his horse the last fifty yards. It came into the yard slinging mud. He was a big, prideful man, Matt Pilcher, red-headed and loud-mouthed. He had a real thick skull, too, Major remembered, for he could recall one time when he'd had to hit Matt twice with a fair-sized club before getting results.

Matt came to a plunging stop. He started to say something and then he saw Lafait and looked startled.

" 'Lo, Matt," Lafait said quietly.

"Yeah." Matt looked at Major. "So you sent for him, huh?"

Some folks just naturally had ways of saying things to make your back hair bristle up. "He's here, if that's what you're trying to say." Major looked at the wagon. "Couldn't you get off the road any farther?"

"The old bastard's horses are barely able to haul that wagon on dry ground. I had to try a new place," Matt said.

The scraggly team wasn't much, Major had to allow. The wagon was stuck right now. Matt spun his horse and rode down to the edge of the grass, yelling, "Whip them damn crowbaits, Luke! Keep 'em moving."

Mark and Luke, the next oldest Pilchers by the first marriage, splashed over beside the team, yelling *hah!* and beating the horses with their ropes until the tired animals pressed once more against their harness and pulled the wagon to firm ground at the edge of the meadow.

"You couldn't tie on and pull, huh?" Major said, as Matt came riding back to the yard.

"For that layout? Hell! You and Lafait was too easy with them before, or we wouldn't be having to run them out of the country now." Matt directed his talk to Major but he kept watching to see how Lafait was taking it.

There were seven younguns in the wagon, none of them very far along in years. The oldest was a skinny boy about fourteen who kept staring at Major. Mrs. Rusk, broad-faced, with a slash mouth, held one child in her lap. She looked straight ahead from under her sunbonnet.

Lonzo was a tall, hatchet faced man who sat quietly with a dark kind of patience. Starting with him, the whole passel showed more than a fair dash of Indian blood.

All the Pilchers left the wagon and came crowding into the yard. They jostled their horses around and stared at Lafait. Most of them said some kind of hello, but only Chunk and Burt got down to shake hands with him. They were the two oldest boys by Ross' second marriage, light complexioned, quiet looking. It was said they came by their quietness honestly because they seldom had a chance to get in a word around their red-headed half brothers.

"Where you taking those people?" Major asked.

"We're seeing that they get clear to hell and gone out of our end of the valley," Luke Pilcher said. "They tried to squat on some of Mark's land."

There wasn't much choice among the three red-headed Pilchers. Matt was the biggest and maybe the loudest, but the three of them looked pretty much alike and generally acted alike. Come to a skull and knuckle fight with one, you had to take on all three.

It was a prime wonder, Major thought, that Mark had ever discovered that anyone was squatting on land he claimed, since it was a long way from the main den of the Pilchers. The whole tribe lived together in one place that was beginning to look like a small settlement. For miles around they had taken up claims for every male in the family, including younguns.

To make things look half-way lawful, they had built shacks of a sort in a dozen places. Now and then they rode around and spent a night or two in the shacks, so it would appear that someone was really living on the claims. Any newcomer seeking a place to roost had to be a good many miles from the Pilchers' headquarters in order to find a spot that was unclaimed by some member of the clan.

Since they rode in a bunch, bristling with pistols and rifles, and made a lot of noise, and had a very loose regard for any fixed boundary lines of any given claim, they had been able to convince would-be settlers that free land just didn't exist for about four or five square miles from Pilcher Town, as Jim Goodwin called their main place.

But the pot could not call the kettle black. And the Pilchers were neighbors. And the Rusks had to be considered trespassers. Still, it was an insult to all human beings when people drove others by force.

Mad at the Pilchers because they had dragged the situation right into his yard, Major walked down to the wagon, without any intention of doing anything to change what was happening, but he did want to show in some way that he wasn't happy to see the Rusks pushed from pillar to post.

Lonzo looked at him with bleak hostility. Major stared at his mangled ear. It was a shapeless, ugly mass of red flesh. Lafait's bullet had done that to him.

"Where have you been since last summer?" Major asked.

"Lumbering. Up to the mines," Lonzo said.

"Have you got vittles?"

The younguns perked up, their dark eyes

swinging from their pa to Major, and when Pa didn't answer, one of the little ones said, "We been hungry, mister. We been—"

"You shut up, Benny!" the oldest boy said savagely. He glared at Major. "We don't need nothing from no Whitlock."

"That's right, Miami," Mrs. Rusk said. Her dark stare was set on Lafait.

Matt yelled, "You're wasting our time, Major, unless you want to finish the job of taking 'em on down to your step-pa, since he's always yelling for more people to come in and settle."

So that was what the Pilchers had in mind, Major thought. He knew he should step aside without another word, but he felt sorry for the Rusks and he felt a need to do something to show his sympathy.

"Git on, Lonzo," Mrs. Rusk said. "There's a bad smell here."

Lonzo whacked the team. The horses lurched ahead and one of the younguns tumbled over backward. A long groan of anguish came from somewhere in the wagon box.

"Who's that?" Major said.

Mrs. Rusk's look was a slash of pure hatred. "What the hell do you care?"

There must be a hurt youngun laying in the wagon, Major thought. He walked along beside it and peered over the sideboard. Such a strew of younguns and camping stuff was flung about in the wagon that he didn't see the old man for a moment or so.

Rusk younguns were might nigh tromping all over him as he lay there on a pad of ragged quilts, a beardy old grandpa with a hawk nose, knobby cheekbones, and staring eyes.

"What ails him?" Major asked.

Lonzo kept on driving.

"Stop the wagon, damn it!"

"Leave that wagon be!" Matt shouted.

Major ran forward and grabbed the cheek strap of the nigh horse and stopped the team. "What ails him?"

"Fever." Lonzo waved his arm disgustedly at the Pilchers. "I told them he wasn't fit to be hauled around."

"He never would've got any better if we swallered that story," Luke said.

Major walked back and pushed a youngun aside to look into the wagon again. The old man's eyes were fever wild. One hand pawed aimlessly at his face, then slid away and fell against the dirty bare foot of the boy called Miami.

"Watch he don't grab your leg, Miami," a youngun said. "He's got fearful strength sometimes."

Chunk Pilcher looked into the wagon. "I tried to tell Matt he was awful sick, but—"

"You tried to tell me!" Matt cursed. "You're always trying to tell me. I say he ain't so sick but what he can stand a few more miles."

"This man is near dead!" Major cried. "You're not jouncing him no farther in this wagon."

"Good! We'll give him to you, along with the whole kit and caboodle of Rusks." Matt grinned at his brothers. "Old Maje, he's got lots of land he can't use."

Lonzo tossed the lines to his wife, climbed over the seat, shoved younguns out of the way, and helped Chunk Pilcher and Major get the old man out of the wagon. He was heavier than Major had thought. The burn of fever came through his clothes where their hands touched him.

Chunk and Major carried him into the cabin and put him on Major's bed. "Watch him a minute," Major said.

He went out and told Lonzo, "You folks can stay here until your—"

"Hell with you." Lonzo whacked the team into an uneven start.

Mrs. Rusk's eyes burned with dark fire as she looked back at Lafait still sitting on the chopping block. "Your day will come, you murdering bastard," she said.

Whooping and laughing, the Pilchers escorted the Rusks on their way, beating the team with their ropes when the horses faltered on the steep south hill.

Chunk came from the cabin. "I tried to give him some water. He knocked the dipper hell-west-and-crooked." He got on his horse. "He had a rifle gun and a fair-looking gray horse." As soon as he said it he looked like he wished he'd kept still. Like he didn't care whether or not he caught up, he went trailing after the rest of the Pitcher tribe.

Suddenly Major felt uneasy. "Doggone, them Rusks was unusual agreeable about leaving their grandpa, wasn't they?"

"He ain't their grandpa," Lafait said.

"How do you know?"

"He wasn't with them when we saw them before."

"That don't prove he ain't their kin."

"Maybe so." Lafait shook his head. "But the way they dumped him proves he's got smallpox —or something."

"Oh Christ! You think he does?"

Lafait shrugged. "They got rid of him like he had some kind of plague. The way old Lonzo went over that seat . . . I'll bet he never moved that fast before in his life."

"Well . . ." Major said. He walked toward the cabin and Lafait rose and followed him.

The old man was thrashing around, mumbling and groaning. Lafait leaned close, sniffing like a hound dog. "I don't see no red spots, but I'm itching like I had pits all over me."

They undressed the sick man. He was dry hot, but they didn't find any red spots anywhere. "How soon do they bust out after they take it?" Lafait asked.

"How do I know?" Since Lafait had mentioned it, Major, too, imagined that his face and scalp were itching something fearful. "Let's wash him with cool water."

It took the two of them to get the job done. At times the patient was quiet and unresisting, and then he would start whaling around with his arms like a wild man.

"I'll go get Ma," Major said. "She's had the pox. She'll know what to do."

"I'll go," Lafait said. "I was going anyway."

"All right." Major had to allow that the whole thing was his own doing. Like as not the Pilchers and maybe the Rusks too were laughing at him right now. "The man was dying in that wreck of a wagon," he said defensively.

"Looks like he still is." Lafait put on his coat. "Fine way to come back. I say, 'Hello, Ma, how you been? Get right up to Major's place. He's got a man with smallpox.' "

After Lafait left, the old man was quiet for ten or fifteen minutes.

Major built up the fire and swung the water pot back over the flames, thinking that Ma would likely want some hot water for something when she came. He sure hadn't helped things any by standing against the Pilchers. It wasn't that he didn't favor the idea of making squatters get off the land that was already taken, but it was the way the Pilchers went at things

Those poor old broke-down horses, and all the kids that weren't responsible for what their pa did, and the sick man who was getting tromped and jounced to death. . . . *Major's got lots of land he can't use.* That remark of Matt's kept coming back to mind and it didn't set easy.

The patient tried to rear up and get out of bed, and Major had his hands full for a while. Then the old man's strength ran out and he was limp, with his breathing all raspy. Any minute Major expected his wind to go rattly in his throat. While he had a chance Major kept sponging his arms and face with water.

It seemed to be having a good effect, but all of a hellish sudden the old man lashed out and spilled the basin of water all over Major's chest. As Major clutched at the pan, the patient smacked him a heavy rap in the nose.

"Goddamn the Pilchers!" Major cried.

"Shoot low, you thieving bastards, shoot low!" the old man roared, and that was the only understandable sentence he said during the longest morning Major ever put in.

He was so busy wrestling with the patient that he didn't hear Ma when she pulled up in her light spring wagon along about noon. The sight of her, sure-moving and steady-eyed, was a big relief. "Get the clean bedding and the other things in the wagon," she said.

Major was glad to get out of the cabin. He saw

Lafait riding away to the north. "Where you going, Lafait?"

Lafait waved and trotted on.

"He hasn't got the pox," Ma said when Major went inside with clean blankets wrapped in white canvas.

He didn't ask how she knew; he was content to believe her.

"Where's Lafait going?" he asked.

"Unwrap those blankets and help me get this bed fit for a human being." Ma threw the twisted, water sodden covers on the table. "At least there'll be one bed in the place that doesn't look like boars have been sleeping in it."

"I been figuring to straighten up things, once I got a little time. I—"

"Turn him on his side."

Ten minutes later the old man was resting easy. Ma was spooning some kind of hot tea into him and he was taking it greedily. "You put plenty of water on him and on everything else in the cabin," Ma said. "What he wanted most was a little inside him."

"What's he got?"

"I don't know."

Ma kept spooning away until the patient would drink no more. He fell asleep. "Lafait went up to Pilcher Town to see about a horse and a rifle gun."

Major shook his head. That was Lafait for you. He'd gone churning away like a bull busting a fence, over a trifle, but it hadn't worried him a damn bit that folks might be figuring to steal Deer Valley.

Ma read his thoughts. "Don't you fault him, Major. Just thank the Lord that he's back unharmed. He wasn't born to fight the land any more than your Uncle Lafe was—or a passel more of Whitlocks I could call to mind."

"Did he say anything about leaving?"

"No, and nothing about staying either." Ma turned sidewise in her chair to get a good bearing on Major. "Don't figure to use Lafait for your own selfish ends."

"That's up to him to decide."

Ma shook her head. "Not if you don't want it that way." She paused. "I know about them two men in Texas, Major."

"How'd you find out?"

"Lucinda Burnine told me." Ma's face showed a wondering kind of sadness. "Five men dead for trifling reasons."

"They all tried their best to kill Lafait first!"

"One dead man is enough to give a person a bad reputation," Ma said. "No use to talk, people are afraid of Lafait. Trouble comes to him like new sawdust brings hornets. You're figuring to use him like a mean dog guarding a smokehouse."

"It's his land too!"

Ma shook her head, watching Major with a sharpness that always made him look inside himself. "We took a big chance coming out here to get land," Major said. "You might say that the reason Pa died was—"

"Don't give me any big-mouth talk about the reasons for men dying. I heard all that during the war. Kill all the men you want to in order to hang onto Deer Valley. You do that, Major, but don't ever give me any pious talk about why you did it. You're trying to straddle three claims, and maybe your legs ain't long enough to do it. Just don't you drag Lafait into it. He's got enough to live down."

"I'll straddle 'em some way," Major growled. He went outside and took a long look at the valley. Both Lafait and Ma were right. Deer Valley didn't belong to the Whitlocks, but to him alone.

Of course Ma didn't mean it about killing all the men he wanted to. Damn! Maybe there was some way to make things work out without even thinking about killing anyone.

He took care of Ma's horse and went inside again. She was bathing the old man's wrists. "I took him for kin of the Rusks," Major said. "Did they know him?"

"No. His horse brought him into their camp. He was out of his head then." With a snap of her wrist Ma knocked down a bee that had swept in through the open doorway.

Major stepped on the insect as it twisted and

31

buzzed angrily on the dirt floor. "I'm not the only one who's grabbed more land than the law allows. Look at Burnine and the McAllisters and Tad Sherman. If we stick together—"

"Hogs generally don't."

"They're all friends of ours!" Major protested.

"And you're my son, which ain't changing the mortal fact that you're a hog too."

"What do you want me to do? Give away two claims?"

"I don't know," Ma said quietly.

For the first time Major realized that she was bitterly worried. "Doggone it, Burnine told me there was nothing to worry about. He said—"

"Then why is *he* worried?"

"Him?"

Ma gave Major a long look. "About half the time he doesn't even sleep in the house at night."

Burnine scared? Why, he was the first settler in the whole area. He was about as tough as they came. "I haven't been down that way for a couple of weeks, I guess," Major said lamely.

"It's been two months since you were at Burnine's. Lucinda told me."

"I've been busy." Major could not explain why, but it always fretted him to be away from Deer Valley any longer than absolutely necessary.

The sick man began to thresh around and Ma had to give all her attention to him. After she got him quieted, she turned to Major. "I'm afraid things are going to boil over in this country. So is Goodwin, but he won't take time to admit it."

"On account of us hogs?"

Ma nodded. "I can't fault you for wanting all of Deer Valley, but I will blame you if you kill to keep it. I'll tell you right now that you'd better find some way to hang on without using a rifle gun. You're alone here, Major."

"You're counting Lafait clean out, I see."

"I am. And by the way, you never did promise me about him."

"All right, all right! I won't get Lafait into no trouble over this place."

Chapter Three

Riding toward Little Creek to see Burnine, Major took the old buffalo trail that ran through the foot-hills west of the wagon road. He felt a little guilty about running off the morning after getting Ma to take care of the sick man, but she had urged him to go and find out for himself what was boiling up.

He was crossing a broad gulch about a quarter mile from Kettle Drum Springs, where Brent Lavington had taken up ground, when the quick forward-cock of Smoke's ears warned him of something ahead.

After a few moments he made out the forelegs of a horse standing in the dense pinons across the gulch. One of the Lavington boys, he guessed. They spent a lot of time traipsing the hills.

"All right over there!" Major yelled. "I see you."

"You didn't until your horse told you!" a voice taunted. Polly Lavington was laughing as she brought her little blue roan pony out of the trees with a rush. For a moment Major thought she was going to crash smack into Smoke, who started to sidle, but at the last instant she swung the pony and stopped.

She was about nineteen, Major guessed, but sometimes she acted like she was closer to twelve, jumping out at folks that way and laughing like she didn't have a fret in the world.

"Did I scare you, old sobersides? You look like a crock of curdled milk."

"You didn't scare me none."

Major guessed he looked just the way he felt. Sour. He'd never seen but one other woman who wore men's clothes, and that one had been a tobacco-chewing, loud monster of a female working on the big ferry boat that had brought the Whitlock wagon across the Mississippi.

"Why'nt you dress like you ought to?" Major grumped.

Polly laughed. "You sound like a preacher. Are you really, deep down in your heart?"

"Never you mind." Jeem's cousin! She sure could torment a person and make his thoughts wander, not that it wasn't sort of pleasant to be pestered by her.

She was a leggy woman, for sure. Like a young colt, only there was nothing knobby about her. She was all smooth and willowy and springy and she rode her pony like she'd been born on it. Her hair was as dark as Lafait's. Just about as wild too, chopped off in front to keep it out of her eyes and whacked in back like an Indian's. It wasn't straight though, but kind of fluffy on both sides of the natural part and curling up at the chopped-off ends.

By gosh, that was no way for a woman to keep her hair, though Major had to admit that he sort of liked it.

"Where are you riding today, Major?"

Her eyes were gray as aspen smoke, level and serious as sin one instant, and then they could be full of the devil an instant later. Her mouth was like that too, Major thought. It wasn't small and prissy by no means, but sort of long, with the lips tending toward thinness. She could be solemn as a hooty owl, and then her mouth would crink up at the corners and her white teeth would flash and the little devil imps would shine in her eyes and she would laugh with the purest enjoyment Major had ever heard.

No matter what she wore, you just couldn't think no bad of Polly. Being prim and proper wasn't her way.

If she was bounden to wear pants though, she ought not to be stealing them from her little brother, because he was by no means round where she was round. They were too downright snug where she sat. That kind of thing was apt to disturb a person.

"Has the cat got your tongue, Preach?" Polly made a face at him.

"You stop that preacher stuff," Major growled. The way she had of looking at him and teasing him was fair enough to make him want to grab her right out of the saddle and haul her over and start kissing her and keep on kissing her . . . and . . . and likely get the living hell shot out of him by old Brent Lavington before it all wound up.

"I'm riding over to Little Creek, in case you have to know," Major said.

"Are you going to stop and see my pa?"

"I hadn't thought on it. Why?"

"Are you afraid of my pa!" Polly asked. She put her pony beside Smoke as Major rode on toward the low hills on the far side of the gulch.

"No. Why ought I be afraid of him?"

"I just wondered. I can show you how to go clean around the springs without being seen." Polly studied Major with a serious, questioning expression. "If we turn up this wash—"

"I know how to ride around the springs, if I wanted to," Major said stiffly. He struck straight for the trail that led to Lavington's place.

Before they reached the foot of the hill, Polly spun her pony and went racing up the gulch. "Good-bye, Preach!" she shouted.

Major watched her skim away, her black hair bouncing, her slim back straight and easy, and her long legs holding the barrel of the pony like some of the flatland nabobs Major had seen when the Whitlocks first came out of the Kentucky mountains.

It was cool here in the hills above the heat of the valley, but Major felt all hot and tingly. He took off his old slouch hat and rubbed his sleeve across his forehead.

Brent Lavington was a spring steel blade of a man, fair complexioned, with cold gray eyes. He was building a pen for his two milch cows against the hill when Major rode into the yard. He had seen Major when he first broke over the hill, but he hadn't stopped working, and he didn't quit now.

Mrs. Lavington, a dark-haired woman, thin and tall, came to the cabin doorway and nodded to Major, watching him quietly as he touched his hat and said, "Howdeedo, Mrs. Lavington."

There were two boys, Baskerville and Cato, about fifteen and sixteen, but Major saw no sign of them as he rode on across the yard and around the big spring and on to where Lavington was lashing a pole to a post with wet deer hide.

Lavington paused and nodded curtly when Major greeted him.

"I never seen a fence built just like that," Major said, eyeing the rawhide.

"Poor people have poor ways, Whitlock."

"I didn't mean it that way."

Lavington made no comment. He hadn't been stand-offish when he first came to the country, four months before. While his family camped near Goodwin's store, Lavington had ranged around looking for a likely place to settle. He had stopped at Major's place several times, and while he hadn't been an overfriendly man, he had been courteous and decent and even able to laugh when he described how the Pilchers claimed to own everything within a day's ride of their settlement on Pilcher Creek.

After a month of looking for a prime piece of land, and being told that everything he liked was already taken up, Lavington didn't have much humor left. The last few times he crossed Deer Valley, he didn't stop to visit Major.

"You've done a heap of work here, Mr. Lavington," Major said. It was a good, big cabin, made of straight aspens and dirt roofed. The springs were cleaned out and dammed, and the water that used to dribble away down the gulch until it disappeared into the gravel was now ditched around the tow of a hill above a little meadow of native hay.

"Yeah," Lavington said. "I've got four acres of growing land out of a hundred and sixty."

It was like he was accusing Major of being at fault because most of the claim was hills. "It isn't too good, at that," Major said, "if a man figures on cattle."

"I figure on cattle." Lavington's cold look was a challenge.

"Well, I guess there's room for all of us."

"Tell that to all your friends, Whitlock, starting with the Pilchers."

Major rode away.

Three ridges south he saw Polly hiding behind the trees again, and this time he spied her out ahead of Smoke. Major let out a wild yell and sent his horse in a gravel-kicking charge at her hiding place.

She broke out on the other side and ran her pony up the wash, but when she saw that Major wasn't following, she turned and came back. "What's the matter, Preach? Scared to race?"

"If that's all you want, come out on the flats."

Polly laughed and shook her head.

They followed the old buffalo trail to the top of the next ridge, Major in the lead. He would have gone on down the hill but Polly said, "Hold up, you Major, you." She rode around in front of Smoke. "Why are you always in a hurry? You act like a man with his head down, following a plow."

"I can't fool around all the time. I've got business."

"Foof! You can have business when you're old." Polly put her head back, looking at the mountains. "See all those clouds up there and the way the old mountain stands big and proud in the blue sky. Just looking at it, don't you feel something wonderful inside?"

Major stared at the mountains. "They're pretty, yeah. I always thought I'd climb up there someday."

"I have."

"What!"

"All the way up on that big one with the square top. There wasn't hardly any wind at first. I stood on the highest rock I could find. Everything down in this valley was tiny and no-account, but you could see miles and miles in all directions to other mountains everywhere, and when you kept looking and looking, you could see other mountains beyond the far ones, all blue and misty. I stood there on my rock with my arms stretched out. After a while the wind came blowing and then rain whistled down so hard it stung like little rocks. I reached out and tried to grab it and hug it and all the time I was laughing. Then the rain stopped. The sun came back and way off in the west the thunder growled like a toothless old dog sleeping by the fire and dreaming of chasing rabbits."

Fascinated, Major watched her face as she

talked. Her eyes were shining, her lips parted in a half smile, and her whole expression was clean and clear and beautiful.

"Why don't we climb the mountain, Major?"

"Huh? My gosh, Polly!"

"I don't mean right now, but someday. Someday?"

"Sure. I guess so. I always wanted to."

"When? Tomorrow?"

"No! Sometime when I'm not busy."

"Busy with what? You're twenty-one years old, and you act like you own a dozen plantations. Why don't you stop acting like an old grandpa, Preach?" She watched him with a tormenting smile, her gray eyes laughing.

A heap of thoughts, confused and warm, crossed his mind. "I got a long ride ahead of me," he mumbled, and started to leave.

"Go ahead, Preach. Go talk to all the other old men who're scared to death they'll lose some of their precious land. Is that all you ever think of?"

Major reined Smoke around quickly. "How do you know where I'm going?"

"Anyone could guess without half trying."

"That's just what you're doing too—guessing."

"Your brother came home, didn't he?"

She could not have guessed about that. "Sure," Major said, "my brother came home. I've got a sick man at my place and my ma is there taking care of him. I suppose you know all about what's going on, huh?"

"How would I know all that?" Polly wouldn't look him in the eye. She reached out and disentangled a twig from the mane of her pony. "When are we going to climb that old mountain, Major?"

The bad, uneasy feeling was running through Major again. Someone had been watching his place. Her brothers. There was something unsettling in the thought of people spying on you.

"You tell Bask and Cato they'd better watch out."

"Tell 'em yourself."

"I'll do worse than that when I catch them spying on me," Major said, and rode away.

He was working his way through the juniper trees below when Polly yelled at him, "I guess you're not a preacher after all! My ma says preachers can't keep their paws off young women."

It took Major a moment or two to grasp what she had said. When he came out of the trees he looked back at the top of the hill, but Polly was gone by then.

The first thing that usually hit a visitor at Burnine's was the clamor of his four big dogs rushing out, but this time they were not around. Burnine was at a corral saddling a horse. He saw Major before he was clear of the trees, took one step and swooped up a short rifle gun leaning against the corral poles, and then he recognized Major.

A short, dark man, Burnine looked round and tubby, but Major knew the tubbiness was mainly muscle. Summer and winter, Burnine's cheekbones were burned and peeling in little chips of flesh. "Get down and come in, Major. Cindy and the girls will be glad to see you."

"I wanted to talk to you alone, Mr. Burnine."

"I thought you might." Burnine's eyes, already as direct as awl-points, seemed to sharpen even more. "Yes, sir, I thought you'd be along before this." He finished cinching the saddle, and then he walked over to a corral where a young shorthorn bull was standing. "Have a look at him, Major."

As he walked over to the corral, Major kept one eye on the two-story house of axe-chipped logs.

"You can take him any time," Burnine said.

"I can't today. He looks like a prime one."

"Yeah." Burnine put one foot on a corral rail. "Have they started on you yet?"

"Who?"

"The Regulators."

Major shook his head. "Never heard of them."

"I hear Lafait came back from Texas."

"He did." News sure got around fast, Major thought. He felt obliged to add, "I'm not counting on him in case of trouble. He likely won't be here long."

"See that he stays." Burnine scowled. "About ten days ago, a bunch of the newcomers met at

Lavington's and organized what they call a Committee of Regulation. They figure to reshuffle ownership of land in this whole damn country. This ain't no homesteader war, Major. These people know what they're doing. They're people who would be us, if they'd happened to get here a little sooner. They didn't and that's their hard luck."

Major saw quick movement at one of the upstairs windows. It looked like Susan but he was not sure.

"The rightful owners of this country, the Pilchers, the McAllisters, you and Lafait, me, and a few others, have got to stand together," Burnine went on. "Not only do we hold what we've got, but we take as much more as we've got the guts to hold. We do it, Major, or the damned Regulators will do it. Which do you want?"

"I ain't giving up any land." Major hesitated. "Are you sure it ain't just talk?"

Burnine gave him a grim look. "Two days after that committee was formed, all four of my dogs were killed right here in the yard one night. One of my cow camps was burned. I've let it be known that I don't sleep in the house because some sonofabitch may be waiting to take a shot through the window at me. If they know I'm not there, my wife and Susan and the youngsters are safer, so I've been sleeping out like a damned coyote. That's what your friend Lavington and the rest have brought this country to."

Burnine went over to his horse and kneed it in the belly and then tightened the cinch. "We're meeting tomorrow night at eight at the Pilchers. I'll see you and Lafait then." He swung up into the saddle. "Why don't you go in and visit for a while?"

"I've got to get down to the store," Major said. "Who all is going to be at that meeting?"

"The people I mentioned. The Martins too."

Uriah and Eben Martin were tall, dark, hatchet-faced Missourians who lived on a branch of Little Creek. They didn't mix much with other people, Major knew. From what he had heard of them, the Martin brothers spent most of their time hunting and fishing. They owned a few head of cattle and a half dozen fine horses. It seemed odd to Major that the Martins would be interested in Burnine's meeting. They had taken up only one claim, a large part of which was worthless hills, although they had been in the country early enough to have filed on choice bottomland.

"You may as well take a few minutes to visit the women," Burnine said.

"I'm in sort of a hurry, Mr. Burnine."

"Suit yourself," Burnine said curtly. He was still sitting his horse in the yard when Major rode away.

Susan Burnine came out and walked over to her father. She was seventeen, a full formed woman who moved with a quiet grace that always brought a light to her father's eye. Her straight black hair was piled in shining braids. She was a composed, gentle-talking woman, with not even a hint of Burnine's fire in her green eyes.

"He was in a hurry, Susu," Burnine said. "I tried to get him to stay a while."

"Mama says not to worry about trying to get back tonight. We'll be all right."

"I'll be back. I won't come in, but I'll be out here somewhere tonight." The horse wanted to be gone at once, but Burnine reined it around with hard control and sat for a moment looking down fondly at his oldest daughter.

The twins were already rougher than cobs, Burnine thought. They were chips off the old block, and Evlee, the other girl, had a lot of tough practicality in her makeup. Those three would do just fine in this tough country.

Susan was different. Oh, she would get along all right, but she ought to have a chance to know some of the cultural things in life that would be slow in coming out here. He'd have to talk to her mother again about sending Susan to stay with her cousins in Virginia for a year or so. The trouble was, she didn't want to go.

Burnine had never been back to Virginia after his father moved the family to Texas in 1840, when Burnine was twelve; but he guessed that the Yankees hadn't been able to ruin everything there after the war, the way they were trying their best to do in Texas.

"He was in a hurry, that's all, Susu."

"Of course. He always is—lately." With an honest, gentle kind of wonder Susan asked, "Why is that, Papa?"

"He's worried like the rest of us," Burnine said quickly. He knew that was not the answer, and so he added, "Because he's a stubborn young lout, like most fools his age!" Neither was that the answer, though it was the best Burnine could do at the moment.

As her father rode away, Susan Burnine walked slowly back toward the house to let her hastily pinned up braids down and to change back into an old dress again.

Chapter Four

On his way down the river road to see Jim Goodwin, Major veered off his route to the Toby McAllister place to visit a few minutes with his sister Dorcas. No one was at home. Toby probably was in the hills looking after his cows and Dorcas and the baby were no doubt over at her mother-in-law's, a half mile away.

Major had a brief look around the place. Bigger corrals than the last time he'd been there. The meadow fencing toward the river was completed, and the foundation logs for another room on the cabin were laid. That Toby was a pure McAllister, sure enough, when it came to working like a man burying the devil.

Dorcas had done real well to marry him.

The first thing Major saw when he came up from the creek bottom near Goodwin's was the Rusk wagon, in camp with two other wagons at the spring near the store. More settlers, he thought sourly. Goodwin was a dandy for encouraging folks to stay in the country.

As Major rode past the camps around the spring, he saw Lonzo in conversation with four men. Lonzo broke off his words, glared at Major, and then said something in a low voice that caused the other four to stare. Mrs. Rusk didn't care who heard her. She straightened up from a cooking fire and said loudly, "Take a good look, you men. That's Major Whitlock. He's one of the greedy bastards Lonzo's been telling you about. Mark him well."

Some of the younguns laughed and hooted. The boy called Miami, sharp-faced with an old-man look, picked up a rock and tossed it in his hand, grinning. Major fully expected him to throw it, but he turned his head and rode on.

"Look out!" a youngun shouted, and Major barely kept himself from ducking. When he looked back, making a slow, easy movement of it, the boy was still holding the rock.

Old Jed Caldwell was behind the whiskey-end

of the plank counter, dipping a measuring stick into a keg. "Just a minute," he said. "I'm trying to find out how much them Pilchers drank."

Though he was only about forty, his hair was solid gray and he was stooped, but above an enormous pocked nose, his brown eyes were bright and young.

"Where's Goodwin?" Major demanded.

Jed squinted at the stick. "They swallowed a plenty, I'll tell you." He looked at Major. "You sore about something?"

"Where is he?"

"Well, he was out checking supplies in the big cellar, last I seen of him. How's the sick—"

Major was already at the doorway. He strode outside just in time to see Miami jab a long stick into the flank of Smoke. The horse snorted, kicked wildly and ran down the hill toward the river. Miami's back was to Major. "That'll give him something to do," the boy said, and then he saw the look of alarm on the faces of the younguns who had come along to see the fun.

Miami looked over his shoulder. He started to run but he was too late. In two long jumps Major had him by the galluses.

"Leggo, goddamn you!" Miami said. He had a wiry, twisting strength that was hard to hold, clawing, biting, kicking, until Major pinned his arms and picked him up bodily.

"Hey!" Lonzo yelled.

"The bastard's killing Miami!" Mrs. Rusk shouted.

Lonzo and two of the men at the spring came on the run. "Take your hands off that boy!" Lonzo said.

Major let Miami down, holding him by the shoulders. "One of us is going to whale the daylights out of him, Rusk, for running my horse off. You or me. Which way do you want it?"

Lonzo transferred his anger to the boy in an instant. "Did you do that, Miami?"

"Sure, I jabbed his horse with a stick. I'll do it again too!"

"Gawdamighty!" Lonzo groaned. "You been nothing but grief and trouble from the day you was borned. Come here!"

Major let Miami go and gave him a shove toward his father. Lonzo was reaching out to grab him, but Miami ducked his head and charged like a billy goat. He butted his father in the stomach and Lonzo let out a long-drawn *ummnnm* as he doubled over.

Miami was gone before Lonzo got his wind back, and then the father gasped, "Come back here, you no-good little bastard!"

"You ain't beating me, you old sonofabitch!" Miami shouted.

"Give me a horse, somebody!" Lonzo bawled. "I'll run that youngun down and tromp him into the ground!"

"Leave him be," Mrs. Rusk said.

Lonzo turned on her savagely. "Woman, keep your big mouth shut or I'll roll you end over end!"

Mrs. Rusk brandished a piece of firewood. "Come on!" she screamed. "Help yourself, you old goat!"

It had been in Major's mind to demand that his horse be caught and returned, but as the Rusks began to quarrel, he decided that he'd got out of the mess well enough. He glanced at Miami, standing fifty yards away, ragged, defiant, wild as a young wolf. For a moment the boy reminded him of Lafait at the same age.

Drawn by the shouting, Goodwin was coming up from the hillside cellar. Major met him and said, "Nothing but a family fight." He looked disgustedly toward the Rusks. "What for are you letting them hang around here, anyway?"

"Oh?" Goodwin gave Major a calm look. He was a big man, with a strong, clean-cut brown face. Though Major by no means could think of him as a father, even after Goodwin and Ma got married, he knew that the storekeeper was about as fine a friend as any man would ever find.

The trouble was—and that was what was eating Major now—maybe Goodwin was so darned big and friendly in his thinking that he was helping ruin the country.

"Why am I letting them hang around?" Goodwin repeated. "Come on."

Major followed him down to the cellar, a cool, gloomy dugout with rock walls laid without mortar. The heavy timber roof was covered with three feet or more of earth. Barrels and bales and sacks of merchandise were stacked on log runners along the back wall.

"Yeah, them and the others you're always telling to settle," Major said. "Damn it, the country is getting all jammed up with people."

Goodwin cut shards of plug tobacco into his palm. He rubbed the pieces between his hands and filled his pipe. He took his time tamping the tobacco and lighting his pipe. "Too many people in the country already, eh?"

"It's getting that way almighty fast!"

"How's the sick man?"

"He was better, after Ma got there. What I came to—"

"How long will she be gone?"

"She said to tell you three, four days. You want to talk to me or not, Mr. Goodwin?"

"I suppose you mean about the Committee of Regulation?"

"Sure. Where do they get the right to divide the land the way they see fit?"

"They have no such right," Goodwin said, "any more than others had the right to take more land than the law allows, in the first place. What we've got to do is head off the trouble that's already started."

"What do you mean, 'we'?"

"You're smack in the middle of it, Major," Goodwin said. "I advise you to do this, and don't waste any time doing it: find two people you can trust. Put them on those two claims that are filed now under your brothers' names. They must actually live there, understand, and improve the land. Later, you can buy their relinquishments or, if they stay the full five years and get a patent, you can buy their titles."

"That sounds like a heap of trouble," Major said. The biggest problem, right at the start, would be finding two people he could trust to return the land to him.

Goodwin acted like it was settled. "That'll take care of your main worry, and it should keep the Committee of Regulation from bothering you. The same thing won't work so well with Burnine and with the Pilchers because there aren't enough people in this whole valley to hold down the land they're laying claim to."

"Saying your idea works," Major said cautiously, "that still won't give me any legal hold on a place to run my cows. I sure can't keep a thousand cows on three quarter sections."

"A thousand cows, by Jonah!" Goodwin stared at Major. "You have grown some, haven't you?"

"I'll have 'em in time."

Still staring, Goodwin nodded slowly. "I believe you, Major, but I can't tell you any way to own enough land to run that many head on. There's no need to own rangeland. You can use it."

"Suppose everyone else thinks the same way?"

"Some of that problem will adjust itself naturally. Some people won't have guts enough to try cattle. Some of them won't be willing to work at it. Some will fail when they try. There are lots of reasons why every settler here isn't going to go into cattle. You're thinking up problems that don't exist."

"Lavington said he was going to run cattle."

"All right, all right. Do you want to deny him the right to try?"

"I don't suppose I do." Major remembered that he'd once told Lavington there was room for everyone, but now he wasn't so sure about that.

"I'm doing what I can to get folks started in different things," Goodwin said. "Take the Rusks—I've got a sawmill in Denver right now. Lonzo is going to run it for me, as soon as I can get it here and set up. That's what he used to be— a sawyer. Lumber will help build a town. A town attracts people, businesses, lawyers, doctors, all kinds of people.

"Why we haven't even got started in this country, Major. Mining has only been scratched at. There's timber to last for centuries. There'll be ditches built to reach some of the dry land, and then no telling what crops can be raised. Then we'll have a railroad, and then . . ."

Goodwin went too far and too fast for Major to follow. The present was all Major wanted to worry about. Towns, railroads, folds swarming around like ants—all that didn't interest him.

". . . So you see, it won't be all cattle, Major. There'll be developments here that we can't even guess at now. What we've got to do is work together, all of us, the best way we can, and in the long run we'll come out all right."

No use talking, Goodwin had the words and a way of using them, with his face alive and his hands whacking the air. And you couldn't say he was just dreaming things, because he worked hard to make them come about.

"We don't have to fight a war here," Goodwin said. "I think enough people can be convinced that there are other ways to settle a dispute. Now, when you go to that meeting with the Pilchers and the others tomorrow night—"

"You know about that."

Goodwin gestured with his pipe. "They made no bones about it. They were here all night. They left about a half hour before you came to go see Shad McAllister. Old Shad has sort of been straddling the fence."

Not according to Burnine, Major thought. Tarnation! There were so many different opinions floating around, a man couldn't be sure what anyone was thinking.

"What I started to say, Major, when you go to

that meeting, try to talk peace. They respect you, and—"

"I ain't sure that I'm even going to that meeting. Right now I'm going home and think about this whole thing and maybe figure what I'm going to do."

Goodwin shook his head gravely. "There's no way for you to stay clear. You're going to wind up on one side or the other, whether you like it or not."

"We'll see," Major said stubbornly.

At the store he loaded a tote sack with staples that he had run out of at home, and a few items that Ma had told him to get.

At Chico Brush Creek, five miles from the store, Major came upon the group watering their horses. The big pool, which would dry up entirely before fall, was in the cottonwoods a hundred yards off the road. Major didn't know anyone was there until after he had turned off the road and was almost to the trees.

He heard Fred Grosland say, "It's still a hell of a long ride just to look after someone as worthless as them Rusks."

Harve Stenhouse answered in his deep voice, "We've got to treat everyone alike, or we don't get everybody's support."

"Ho!" Major yelled.

He rode on to the waterhole.

No one spoke to him. The whole passel of men

strung out around the water looked at him with suspicious, half angry expressions. They didn't like being surprised, and Major could see they were fairly busting to know how much of their talk he had overheard.

Fred Grosland and his two sons gave Major the sourest looks of all. It was easy for them, since their main features were jammed together in the middle of their moon faces, as if the Maker had misfigured how much room there was to work with. Ma had always said that, at their best, the Groslands looked like they had upset stomachs.

Big Harve Stenhouse had just finished drinking from the trickle of water that came down over black rocks at the head of the pool. His face was wet and he didn't bother to wipe at it, but just stood there staring at Major from bright blue eyes, with a little dab of green moss speared on the sandy bristles of his chin.

Joe Bob, Harve's gangling son, who was about Major's age, had stayed at Deer Valley many times. He and Major were pretty good friends. Now Major started to speak to him and almost did, but before the words became sounds, Joe Bob turned away with a sullen look and began to fiddle with his saddle.

That brought the bristles up on Major's neck. To hell with Joe Bob Stenhouse; to hell with them all.

Major got down and led his horse toward the

pool, and Brent Lavington pulled his horse over to make room.

Of course it was no surprise to see Lavington there. They all must have had some kind of meeting cooked up beforehand, Major guessed, and then those who hadn't known about the Rusks had been told, and now the whole bunch was going down to Goodwin's to hear Lonzo's story.

Lavington said, "Let's get on, boys." He was the last one to mount. He kept fooling around with his cinch until all the others were leaving the grove.

Major said, "If you're fretting about the Rusks, there's no need. They're all right. I just seen them."

"You call being herded like cattle all right?" Lavington said it and then his expression changed and he looked like he wanted to say something more friendly, but he glanced at his companions and was silent.

Then Big Harve bellered for Lavington to come on, and the man turned from Major suddenly, got on his horse and rode away.

Now that he had seen the Regulators face to face, he was not nearly as worried as before. Most likely they had just had a meeting at Kettle Drum Springs. They hadn't liked it much when he rode in on them unexpectedly, but that was only natural.

Let them have their damned committee and fancy themselves as somebody's guardian angels.

On the south mesa Major reined in to sit a spell and look at Deer Valley. Smoke was rising from the cabin chimney. In the upper meadow he saw his oxen, Fawn and Steuben, and a gray horse he had never seen before.

Chapter Five

"His name is Smith O'Neal," Ma said.

The sick man was still flat in bed but his eyes were clear and aware. "I'm beholden to you and your ma, Whitlock. Come tomorrow, I'll be on my way."

Ma was sitting by the fireplace in a rocking chair. A suit of Major's ragged underwear lay across her lap. "We'll see how you feel in the morning, Mr. O'Neal."

"Where were you heading?" Major asked.

O'Neal grunted. "Hard to say."

Behind the gray whisker stubble, the gauntness and the pallor, Major saw a heap of toughness in O'Neal's face. He dozed off before Major could ask another question.

"That was no trifling fever," Ma said. "He won't be going nowhere for four or five days." She held up the garment she was patching. "If that ain't something."

"I was going to do something with it, as soon—"

"Burning would have been about right. How was Dorcas?"

"She wasn't home." In the corner by the fireplace Major saw a Sharps eight-sider. He examined it, admiring the curly maple stock inlaid with silver and turquoise. "Where did Lafait go after he picked up this and the horse?"

"Dancing—him and Bill Gifford. They—"

"That Gifford," Major growled. "I wish Lafait would stay clean away from him. Here he's barely home and he's off running around with that no-good already."

"How was Susan?"

"Didn't see her. I had business with her father, not her. Burnine is fighting mad, I can tell you."

"So will the Pilchers be when they get home."

"You mean Lafait— What did he do when he got this rifle?"

"Not Lafait," Ma said. "Ross Pilcher didn't fuss about giving up the horse and the rifle gun." She put down the sewing and looked at Major quietly. "Somebody went around today and burned all those little claim shacks the Pilchers had."

The Regulators, Major thought. So that was what had brought the whole bunch of them up in this end of the valley. All his hopeful thinking about there being no real bad trouble was dead now. "That was a fool thing for them to do!"

"For who to do?" Ma asked quietly.

"The Regulators."

"Who are they?"

"I could guess real close," Major said.

"I can beat that. Your Regulators, as you call them, rode across the west meadow on their way home. I saw them."

"Harve Stenhouse, Joe Bob, the Groslands—you seen them?"

Ma nodded.

"Brent Lavington?"

Ma frowned. "No, I don't recall seeing him."

"Did they see you?"

"I misdoubt they did. I was hanging up blankets out in the trees, so I just stood quiet and watched them. Not that I care if they did see me."

Major said, "I met them face to face at Chico Brush."

"Ah!" Ma picked up her patching. "Are you going to name them to the Pilchers?"

"No."

"Why not?"

"I'll take care of myself! The Regulators ain't hurt me none." But damnation, why had they torn things wide open before Major had a chance to find someone to hold down his extra claims in Deer Valley. "Who told you about the burning—Lafait?"

Ma nodded.

"Where'd you say Lafait went?"

"Him and Bill Gifford took the two oldest Broome girls and lit out for a dance at one of those mining places up the river." Ma made it sound real sinful. She didn't hold with the hell raising that was said to go on in mining camps.

Major slept that night in the bunk across the room from O'Neal, while Ma took Dorcas' bed in the loft. It seemed to Major that he had barely fallen asleep when shouts and the pounding of hooves roused him.

He leaped out and groped toward the rifles above the fireplace. At the same time he heard a thump and a curse as O'Neal, who had struggled out of bed, collided with the table and fell across it.

Horses came thundering into the yard. Someone whooped and fired a shot. And then Major recognized Matt Pilcher's drunken laugh.

"My rifle," O'Neal said. "Where's my rifle?"

"It's nothing but a bunch of drunken idiots," Major said disgustedly. He helped the old man back into bed.

"Ole Maje goes to bed with the chickens!" Matt Pilcher shouted.

"You reckon we all ought to go in and see him?"

"He wouldn't have a drink, not him!"

"If he had a still in there, he wouldn't offer nobody one little drink, not old Maje!"

"Spread out as far as you, boys!" Matt yelled. "Let's try to find the road across that valuable meadow of his!"

Whooping, firing their pistols, the Pilchers rode on.

The bastards, Major thought. They wouldn't be laughing near so loud when they got home and found out what had happened to their claim shacks.

Surprisingly, O'Neal was strong enough in the morning to dress and go outside, where he sat in the sun for a half hour before Ma made him go back to bed. "How old are you?" she asked.

"I never tried to keep track. I was seventeen, or thereabouts, when I first went up the Missouri with a bunch of trappers in '23 or '24."

After dinner Major stuffed some biscuits in his pocket and said, "I'm going up and see about my cows. I'll likely be gone long after dark, so don't worry."

Ma nodded thoughtfully. "That's what you want me to tell Burnine and the others when they come by here this afternoon on their way to the big meeting at Pilchers?"

"Tell 'em you don't know where I went."

As he rode along the north mesa, Major thought of how snugly Deer Valley could be sealed off by having two more claims. But four forties on the north mesa and string another one-hundred and sixty acres in forties along the south mesa. . . . The land was mostly sage and rabbit brush, but when it rained, the bunch grass did fine.

And by ditching from a good damn high on Deer

Creek, a man could get water to those mesas. Then if he could get hold of everything from the upper end of the valley clear to the mountains. . . . What a patch of land! Not as far as the eye could see but a goodly chunk just the same.

I'll do it, he told himself. Somehow, I'll do it!

Even Lafait didn't know about the small hot water spring in the wooded canyon. Calf Runner had told Major about it one night when the Utes were camped in Deer Valley, and Major hadn't quite believed him, until he found the place himself.

Having a secret hideout appealed to some remnant strain of boyishness that Major seldom allowed to express itself. There was time today, he guessed, to have another look at the hidey hole.

He left Smoke in the aspens and made the plunging descent through tangled brush to the canyon bottom. It was a hot springs of strong-tasting mineral water that came out at the base of a cliff and fell at once into the South Fork of Deer Creek.

Deep carved in the rocky bottom was a pool about twenty feet wide and four or five feet deep.

For a half hour Major sat on a rock and dabbled his feet in the warm water, and then suddenly, as if driven by guilt because he was loafing, he put his socks and boots on and struggled back up the steep side and rode on about his business.

He found his five Shorthorn cows with their

calves in the thick grass of an aspen park. Nine of his Longhorn steers were higher on the skirts of the mountain.

Searching for an hour longer, he found the tenth steer. Magpies and little wolves had been at it for sometime. It had been shot through the neck. About two weeks before, he estimated. Maybe around the time the Regulators organized their committee.

In a cold rage, and with great patience, Major went over the whole area. The only fresh sign in the game trail just above where the steer lay was a sprinkle of deer tracks. The rains had wiped out all the older marks.

All he could make of it was that someone had deliberately killed one of his steers and let it lie.

Major rode home by late starlight. Lafait was in the upper bunk. He muttered sleepily, "Where you been? They missed you at the meeting."

"You were there?"

"Yeah. I'll tell you about it in the morning." Lafait went back to sleep in a matter of seconds.

When Major rose the next morning, O'Neal was already up, sitting on the chopping block, catching the first rays of the sun. Major had to half haul Lafait from his bunk in order to rouse him. "I want to hear about that meeting."

They talked down by the willows while Ma was cooking breakfast.

"Well, there wasn't much to it, mostly a lot of

jawing and yelling," Lafait said. "Me and Gifford just set and listened."

"They must have done something."

Lafait shrugged. "They set up another meeting, that is, in case the Regulators do something in the meantime."

"Is that all?"

"Burt and Chunk got into a pretty good fight with the Apostles. I thought for a minute they were going to win, but old Matt and Mark and Luke ganged up on them and knocked hell out of them."

"What was that about?" Major asked.

"When they voted to hang Lavington, Burt and Chunk were against it, so—"

"Jesus Christ! You mean that bunch voted to hang Lavington?"

Lafait yawned. "Damn, I'm hungry. They voted whether or not to hang him, I meant. It wasn't unanimous, which was what it had to be for it to stick."

"Who started that hanging business—Burnine?"

"Sure."

"Who voted against it?"

"Well . . . let's see." Lafait yawned again. "Besides Burt and Chunk, old Tad Sherman and Shad McAllister. Gifford too."

"How about you?"

"Me? Hell, I don't own land around here. I didn't vote." Lafait laughed. "Old Burnine, he was fit to be tied about the way things went. He made it sound so simple, just hang Lavington and that would put the fear of God in the rest."

Major cursed. "All that would do is blow it wide open."

"Sure, Maje. That's just what's going to happen. One sneak or one hothead is going to kill somebody, and then hell is going to break loose."

Major decided not to tell his brother about the dead steer. There was no telling how Lafait would take it.

Ma called them to breakfast, and as they walked toward the cabin, Lafait said, "Jed Caldwell came by yesterday afternoon. He's going prospecting, so Ma's going back to take care of the store today. Gifford and me are going to Denver tomorrow with Goodwin to get a sawmill."

"Gifford and you! Where's Goodwin figure on getting that sawmill—out of a whorehouse?"

Chapter Six

Near a spring seep not far from where the Rusks had tried to settle, Major and Smith O'Neal built the cabin. O'Neal said he didn't need much of a place. The cottonwood logs they dragged from the grove below with Fawn and Steuben were crookedy and heavy as sin. Major and O'Neal manhandled them into place without barking them and with a minimum of trimming.

O'Neal had a world of raw power in his big frame, and you'd never suspected that he had been nigh on to dying of fever not long before. He grunted and sweated, not talking much, carrying his end of the labor well enough, though Major could tell he didn't give a dang for such work.

Near noon of the third day they had the thing just about licked. It wasn't a very big cabin but O'Neal said it was big enough. When Major said that he had some wagon boards that would make a door, O'Neal grunted and declared that all he needed for a door was a buffalo hide which he'd get in a day or two.

"I don't know where," Major said. "There ain't been no buffalo around here for a long, long time."

O'Neal was stuffing moss and dead grass into the gaps between the poles of the roof. He stopped working suddenly. "There used to be plenty."

Every time thereafter when it seemed that he had recovered from the fever, which was to plague him until the end of his life, he had those lapses of understanding between past and present.

The cabin was stout enough, for the logs were so tarnal heavy that once they were notched and put in place, they were bound to stay. There were no windows and the fireplace of rock and white clay from the hill beside the spring was crudely put together and just about big enough to cook a rabbit.

"I ain't expecting to sit before it in a rocking chair," O'Neal said. "That'll hold enough fire to run you out."

The ridge log was so low that Major's head just missed scraping it. O'Neal was five inches taller, but he said the lack of head room didn't worry him none.

"When I want to stand up, I'll be outside. Do most of my cooking outside too. Most of my sleeping too, less'n it's blizzarding. Wouldn't have to go in then, except I lost two of the best robes that ever was when I was ramming around blind on that last fever spree."

He waved a big paw when they threw the last dirt on the roof. "There she is, Major. Most of the time I'll be leastways around it somewhere, so that ought to hold this claim for you."

The one hundred and sixty ran almost to the Arkansas. Major said, "You're not getting much out of this agreement, Mr. O'Neal." A couple of blankets, Lafait's traps, some food, a few cooking utensils—O'Neal had turned down a large part of the things Major tried to give him to use in the cabin.

O'Neal grunted. "Having land suits some people but it don't shine with me." He looked at the warm pinon hills across the river and there was something in his expression that cut Major clean out, and once more there seemed to be a slipping back in time. "There ain't but very little any man can give me, so don't stew about it."

He wasn't just talking, Major knew; there really wasn't much of anything he wanted. It was a funny way to be, but at the same time Major felt a little envious. "I'm going up toward the mountains to look at my cows." Major sort of hoped O'Neal would say he wanted to go along. He waited a spell but the man didn't show any interest.

Major felt fine as he rode toward home. It had been a prime piece of luck when Lonzo Rusk hauled O'Neal right to his doorway. Now if he could just find somebody to put on the upper claim, not even the Regulators could yell about him straddling too much land.

There had been no more trouble since the Pilchers had their shacks burned. It just might be that the Regulators were kind of scared over what they had done. Maybe they'd got a lot of meanness out of their systems and wouldn't be aching to pry up hell, at least for a while.

Knowing that he would be gone until late, he stopped at the cabin to get a pocketful of biscuits left over from breakfast. He stuffed the biscuits into his pocket, stepped outside and pulled the door to. He'd have to hurry if he wanted—

Something chunked into the log close to his shoulder. An instant later he heard the sharp crack of a rifle. Without thinking, without looking around, he leaped back into the cabin and ran to the buffalo gun on the fireplace rack.

Instinct served him that far, but when the gun was loaded, he began to think of the next step, and that cost him time. He didn't want to go out through the doorway, but both windows were solidly fixed. The idea of smashing one of them didn't set well.

If I just stand here trying to be smart, that sonofabitch will be a mile away before I make up my mind, he told himself.

Major hesitated a moment longer and then he ducked low and ran through the doorway, diving to the ground. It was an awkward move that knocked the wind out of him. He rolled behind the chopping block and lay there gasping until he got air back into his lungs.

Major poked the buffalo gun around the side of the block. A tree on the other side of the yard blocked his view of the mesa. It was fixed in his mind that the shot had come from up there, and then he began to wonder. He could see down the meadow clearly enough, all along the south side of the dense willow growth beside Deer Creek.

From the willows, or from the edge of the mesa?

He scrabbled over to the woodpile. That was better. Now he had a good view of the edge of the mesa. About three hundred yards away he thought he saw a thin puff of smoke wisping away into the sunny air, but as he kept staring hard, he decided that his eyes had tricked him, for he began to imagine that he saw smoke in several places.

There was disgrace in lying trapped in his own yard. He had to move, to find the rifleman. He crawled into the cottonwoods, then rose and walked slowly through the trees, angling up the hill.

A full view of the mesa showed him nothing but sunlight shimmering on sage and rabbit brush. For a mile the land sloped gently toward the mountains. It was farther than that to the red rocks east, at the break above the river, and to the south, nothing but the road disturbed the even plane for two miles.

Say there had been time for a man to have ridden out of sight after firing the shot, there would be dust still hanging in the air. There was none, so the shot must have come from the willows.

For a half hour Major lay at the break of the hill and watched the thickets along Deer Creek. The magpies down there showed no alarm, and all kinds of tweety birds flitting among the willows in search of insects went about their work without avoiding any particular section of the growth.

There was a break in the willows where the road crossed the meadow and an even larger gap about a half mile down the creek. The man must be somewhere in the stretch between the breaks, no matter how the birds were acting.

Some of the clumps of rabbit brush on the mesa were big enough to conceal a man lying flat a hundred yards away; but it just wasn't at all likely that the rifleman had come on foot.

Though he still had his head set on the willows, Major kept one eye on the mesa as he walked. He crossed the road. Two wagons had gone down it that morning, but he and O'Neal had paid them no particular attention.

A hawk circled above him for a while as he made his careful stalk. He passed a badger hole where a coyote had been digging. Its tracks were fresh in the scattered earth. Only the dainty tracks of mice showed in the dust around the clumps of rabbit brush.

He was a full half mile from the cabin when he stopped. From the sound of the shot, he was sure that it had come from a light rifle gun. Looking back at the cabin, he wondered if he could even hit it with the heavy buffalo gun he was carrying.

There was only one thing left, to go down and flush the man out of the willows. Maybe O'Neal would— The thought died unfinished. Looking across the valley, Major saw that O'Neal's horse, which had been near the new cabin, was gone. The old man had ridden off somewhere.

Major charged down the hill on a plunging, zig-zag run. He expected a shot from the willows, but none came. When he hit the meadow, he crawled through the tall grass.

It took him an hour to sweat his way through the dense growth of willows between the lower gap and the road. His clothes were slimed with black mud and his face and hands were snagged and bleeding, and he had seen no sign of any kind to indicate that a man had hidden in the willows.

He grounded the buffalo gun and stood with the sweat hot on his back and arms. It was bad enough to be shot at, but to be shot at by a ghost was a scary thing.

At the cabin he studied the bright mark where the bullet had struck. The course was down-slanting. Hell! If he had been able to study that in the first place, he could have known that the shot had to be from the mesa.

The ball he dug out was about .36 caliber, he estimated. He was tossing the misshapen piece of lead in his hand when he saw the two riders coming from the north. Burt and Chunk Pilcher. They came up from the meadow and he observed that they had their blanket rolls and warbags with them.

"You boys look like you're headed somewhere."

"Yeah," Chunk said.

"I was just before making some coffee."

The brothers glanced at each other. "I reckon we can stay a few minutes," Burt said. He looked at Major's muddy clothing. "You been hand-fishing in the crick?"

"You might say so."

The three of them sat at the long table, drinking coffee, not saying much. "Where you headed?" Major asked.

"Goodwin's," Burt said.

"He's still away after that sawmill."

"We know," Chunk said. "We can wait."

After a time, Major asked, "Trouble at home?"

Chunk blurted it out. "The last quarrel we're going to have with Matt or any of the rest! We're through."

Major weighed it out slowly in his mind. Any Pilcher was the last person in the world he would have figured on to help him hold Deer Valley. Of course Chunk and Burt were not at all like any of their half brothers.

Coming to an understanding with them proved easier than Major had figured. They grabbed at his offer.

"Why, sure," Chunk said, "that'll give us a place to live and we can still work for someone part of the time."

"I'll see that you don't want for vittles," Major said.

Burt shook his head. "We ain't asking that. We can take care of ourselves."

"You understand I'm going to buy the claim from you, if you stay long enough to own it, or else I'll buy your rights to squat, if you leave before the five years?"

"We know what you're doing," Chunk said. "It's

all right with us." He grinned wickedly. "Won't that give old Matt something to think about! He'll be fit to be tied."

That was part of it that was real touchy, Major knew. The rest of the Pilchers, already down on him, would be madder than hornets.

"It'll sort of smash old Matt's big plans to—" Burt didn't finish.

"You mean Matt and the others had some idea of horning into this valley?" Major asked quickly.

Burt nodded. "He talked about it." Neither he nor Chunk would say any more. Major reckoned they were so fresh away from home, maybe they figured they'd be traitors to say too much.

"We can pick a place this afternoon for the cabin," Major said. He already had it picked in his mind. "Tomorrow we can start building it."

As usual, when they had a decision to make, Chunk and Burt stared at each other like wild billy goats. Major never did know how they settled things by just looking at each other, except maybe they had been drawn so close together through years of protecting themselves from their half brothers that they had built up some kind of quick, mysterious understanding.

"We can't do it today," Chunk said.

"We wasn't exactly going to Goodwin's first," Burt added. "We was going to Lavington's. He offered us a job of work. Now we have to go tell him we can't take it."

"Lavington!" Major said. "What kind of work did he have?"

The Pilchers hesitated. "About like we just took from you," Chunk said.

"We didn't make him no promises," Burt added quickly. "We said we'd talk to him, if ever we busted away from home."

"How'd he even know you didn't get along too good at home?"

"Well, we traipse around some in the hills with Cato and Bask Lavington," Chunk explained. "They knew, so I guess they just naturally told their pa."

By Ned, there were a heap of things going on that he didn't know about, Major thought. Here he'd been thinking that the Regulators were just setting around doing nothing since the burnings, and all the time they were figuring pretty slick.

"What land were you going to hold for Lavington?" he asked.

Chunk shrugged. "He never said. He sort of hinted that a lot of folks would be doing the same as us, and that the Regulators would see we didn't get run off."

"You're better off with me here," Major said. "Matt and the others are going to be real sore at you, but it would be a sight worse if you'd took up with Lavington and his bunch."

"That's what we figured," Chunk said, and quick.

"We'll go tell Lavington," Burt said, "and then we'll come right back and be ready to start the cabin in the morning."

After the Pilchers had ridden away, Major sat at the table sketching on a piece of wrapping paper. He decided that it might be best to relocate the upper claim for Burt and Chunk.

He could run two of the forties on the south mesa and swing the other two across the upper end of Deer Valley. After he got it laid out on paper, it was well set in his head. He crumpled the paper and tossed it toward the fireplace.

The wad bounced off the edge of the raised hearth and rolled into the disorderly mess of gear along the south wall of the cabin.

I ought to straighten things up there one of these days, he thought. The table was no great example of good housekeeping, either, what with last night's dirty dishes and the breakfast dishes, along with a few frying pans still scattered around.

He decided to clean things up a little, including himself. Sighing, he picked up the water bucket and stepped outside.

The bullet chunking into the log close to him scared him worse than the first time. He threw the water bucket away and dived back into the cabin. The sonofabitch had done it again!

It was once too often. This time Major had the benefit of experience. He peered around the doorway and marked well the small drift of powder smoke on the edge of the mesa. It was not visible for long, but long enough for him to sight from the edge of the doorjamb to the rocky crest of a hill far away across the river.

Not long afterward, he was walking down the mesa with the buffalo gun in both hands. He crossed the road fifty yards back from the edge of the hill and went on slowly until he thought he had gone far enough. He turned and walked over to the break of the mesa and found that he had gone too far east. Very slowly now he went along the edge until he was dead in line with the cabin and the rocky crest of the distant hill.

This was the place where he had seen the puff of smoke.

There was the badger hole he had seen before. There were his own tracks. A few clumps of rabbit brush. The scattered earth where the coyote had dug. Emptiness. Nothing.

An eerie feeling ran through him. The whole thing was bidding fair to be like something from ghostly black night stories that old men told back in Kentucky. Major swallowed slowly, looking all around him.

He checked his sighting. As far as he could tell, he was lined up all right, but he allowed that he could be off a matter of ten or fifteen feet either way.

Along the hill for at least fifty feet in both

directions there was only bare ground. And yet from somewhere very close to where he stood, a man had fired a rifle gun—and disappeared where there was no place to disappear.

The tiny spot of wetness caught his eye first, just a mite of gleam in the sandy soil at the mouth of the badger hole. He stepped over close to it and then the rest took shape. He saw the roundness of a head pressed hard into the loose earth, almost covered, the face nearly hidden by a clump of rabbit brush that seemed to be growing naturally.

Major's first feeling was one of relief: he wasn't crazy, after all. Anger followed quickly. "Come out of there!"

The man didn't move. He was scooched so deep in the hole that Major knew he was harmless at the moment, and so he squatted down to have a close look at his face. An arm and hand exploded upward, lashing dirt into Major's eyes.

Half blinded, he dropped his rifle and tried to grab the man's arm. The fellow was coming out of the hole like a frantic animal, full of wiry, twisting strength. Major got a grip on him and lost it and he lost his next grab too when cloth tore away from his fingers.

The man almost made it. Squinting through the red pain in his eyes, Major saw him getting away on hands and knees. Major lunged out and got him by the legs. Even then he had a hard time holding him, until he got one arm hooked around the man's neck. Major surged to his feet with the struggling body in his grip.

He blinked away some of the dirt in his eyes and saw what he had captured.

Miami Rusk, the skinny wildcat youngun.

Surprise made Major ease his grip. Miami bit his arm.

"Goddamn!" Major howled. "You tried to kill me!"

"I didn't! All I wanted was to scare you." Miami quit struggling. His laugh was taunting. "You sure crawled around on your belly, didn't you?"

"Why, you little—!" Major bent one leg, threw the boy across it and began to spank him.

Miami twisted down and bit him on the leg. Dirt and sand showered out of the boy's long hair as Major batted him with open hand in the side of the head to knock his teeth loose, and then he began to whale the boy in angry earnest.

Miami relaxed suddenly. "Beat away, you old sonofabitch!"

Major did just that until he was ashamed of himself. Then he jerked Miami to his feet and faced him. There were tears on the youngun's dusty cheeks but his glare was still bitter and unconquered. "Beat some more, you bastard. See where it gets you."

"Why'd you shoot at me?"

"For fun."

"For fun!" Major shouted angrily, and then his

eyes narrowed as he stared at the boy. "Who sent you?"

"Nobody," Miami said contemptuously. "I don't need nobody to tell me how to make you run like a rabbit." Again the boy taunted Major with his laugh. "You scrambled around like a blind dog running into things!"

"I'm taking you to your pa, and—"

"That old sonofabitch, he ain't got nothing to do with me no more. Go ahead and take me."

Major let the boy loose. "Look, Miami, I got nothing against you."

"I got plenty against you."

He was a hard one, sure enough, Major thought, but he was only a youngun. He felt sorry for the boy. "Come on down to the cabin with me, Miami, and we'll talk about why you done this." He took the boy's arm.

"Sure," Miami said, and then jerked away and dived toward the buffalo gun.

He was coming up with it when Major landed on him and knocked him flat. Major twisted the weapon away from him and stood up. "What the hell is the matter with you!"

Miami got up slowly, gasping for air. Fresh tears ran down his face, but his defiant expression didn't change. "You're bigger'n me now, but someday you won't be, you Whitlock bastard."

The boy walked away on the hot mesa, barefoot, ragged, his hair standing in a wild shock.

"Come back here," Major said.

"You'll play hell making me."

Major watched him go, angling up the mesa toward the mountains. He felt sick about the whole thing. A half starved youngun hating him that way. Maybe it went clean back to when Lafait had shot off old Lonzo's ear, but the boy seemed to hate his pa too. . . . Maybe he hated everybody.

Major shook his head. He picked up the buffalo gun and went over to the badger hole. He could see now that Miami had done a power of digging to make himself a hidey hole. Major reached down and pulled out a squirrel rifle, an old, beat-up rusty weapon. He picked up a dented powder flask and a small bag of balls.

There was one other thing, the foreleg of a coyote, with the dried blood still lumpy on the cut-off end.

He looked at the small, straight figure going toward the mountains. He wished it had been a man, and then maybe he could have understood.

Miami Rusk's fifteenth birthday was two days in the past, though Miami did not know that. He sat down in the pinons to rest, rubbing his sore arm and shoulder. That goddamn Major Whitlock had a grip like a bear. He was one mean sonofabitch, but some-day . . . someday. . . .

Old man Lavington might be even meaner when he found out how Miami had used the rifle.

Lavington had taken Miami in after Miami had run off from Pa. Pa was a no-good old bastard, any way you looked at it. He never could make anything work out, and he never fought back when people tromped on him.

"I don't want you to use this to sneak down and take a shot at your pa, you hear?" That's what Lavington had said when he gave Miami the rifle. "You bring in some game and help out with the boys and you'll be earning your keep."

That had been fair enough. Miami hadn't shirked on any part of the agreement. As far as wanting to shoot Pa, hell, he wasn't worth shooting.

It had been fun though to make Major Whitlock crawl around on his belly. Miami had aimed to hit above the doorway. He guessed he had just about done it, too, from the way old Major had jumped.

Getting caught hadn't been much fun, though.

Rubbing his sore shoulder, Miami got up and faded into the pinons like a lean, hungry young animal.

Tomorrow he'd go back and face Lavington. Or maybe he wouldn't go back at all.

He set two rabbit snares that night. In the deep mast under a huge pinon tree he slept comfortably, and when he rose in the morning he had a rabbit. He roasted it and ate it all for breakfast.

It was afternoon before he decided to go back to Lavington's.

Polly was helping her ma wash clothes in the

yard. Miami didn't look directly at her, not even after she said, "Glad to see you back, Miami." He went to where Lavington was trimming logs for a headgate.

Cato and Baskerville were working in the ditch below.

If old Lavington didn't like what he was going to say, he could go to hell, and Miami would leave again. Lavington chunked his axe into a log and sat down, digging in his pocket for chewing tobacco.

"I had me a couple of shots at Major Whitlock with your rifle gun."

Lavington sliced a chaw off the tobacco plug. "So?"

"So I damn right did, that's what!"

"You got something to say, Miami, or do you figure to show me how mean and tough you are?"

Miami hung fire for a moment, mighty close to leaving. Lavington had been fair with him. He hadn't given him no jawing about how to behave and what was wrong with him.

Miami told the whole story.

"You done it just to scare him, huh?"

"Yes, sir."

"Why?"

"He's no good, that's why."

"You didn't do it because you thought you were helping me out some way?"

"No, sir."

Lavington rolled his chew and spat. "Do you figure on something like that again?"

Miami shook his head. "I'll get your rifle back."

"It's your rifle gun. I gave it to you. And it's in the house. Major brought it over this morning." Lavington rose and pulled the axe from the log.

"Huh? He did? What—what did he say?"

"Just what you told me. Now if you're going to stay, get something to eat and then go down and help the boys with the ditch." Lavington went back to work.

Miami was cruel hungry, but he saw Polly going into the house and he knew it would be her who got him some vittles, and being close to her always made him feel nervous and sort of funny. "I ain't hungry," he said, and went down to help Baskerville and Cato.

Chapter Seven

After he found the second dead steer, Major built a lean-to at his hideout in the canyon. It was not far from where his cattle ranged, so by staying nights in the snug shelter, he was able to set an ambush near his cattle at dawn and stay on watch until nightfall.

No one came near them during the week he had been following that routine. On this particular day he had overslept in the cool depths of the canyon, and so he had hurried up to the aspen parks without breakfast.

Now, in the middle of the afternoon, he had gone back to the camp to get something to eat. He was frying bacon when he heard a crashing in the undergrowth on the steep slope. He grabbed up his rifle from the lean-to.

A moment later the intruder came sliding into view.

"Polly! Damn it, you're leaving tracks."

"Well, I can't fly. You sure don't care what kind of hole you fall into, do you?"

"How'd you find me?"

"I saw your horse." Polly looked the lean-to over curiously. "What's this for?"

"I may camp here at times, if everybody in the country don't come falling in on me."

"You're a funny old Major. That's why I like you. You grump and snort and then you have to grin about it."

Sure enough, Major found himself grinning. He felt the tingly feeling coming over him. "What are you doing, ramming around all over the country, Polly?"

"What are you talking about? How far from home am I?"

"Well, not far, but you oughtn't to be running around the hills alone."

"Why not, Preach?"

"You just oughtn't, that's why. You don't ever

wander up around Bill Gifford's, do you? And stop calling me—"

"Handsome Bill Gifford, you mean?"

"Handsome! He looks like a snake."

Polly smiled. "I don't even know where he lives, except what Pa and my brothers say. Of course, I don't have to know. He comes by our house all the time."

Oh, sure. That was Gifford for you. Any place there was a good looking woman. He'd even tried to hang around Susan Burnine but her father had tied a can to his tail pretty quick. Major started to say something more about Gifford and then decided against it. "I've got a bite to eat. Fill that coffee pot if you want coffee."

Polly picked up the pot. "I'm surprised, Major. Joe Bob told me you sometimes went all day without knowing whether or not you'd eaten."

"Joe Bob Stenhouse—I suppose he comes by your place too."

"Why, yes." Polly went toward the pool.

Every young blade in the country seemed to be hanging around Lavington's, Major thought.

"This water is warm!" Polly cried.

"Sure. Get it above the hot springs."

"What hot— Oh, I see it now. Well, I declare!"

Major watched her pick her way up the creek. Those britches of Cato's she was wearing. . . .

They ate sitting on a log near the lean-to. "This is a really beautiful place," Polly said. "So green

88

and quiet. Why, it could be a million miles from anywhere."

"I hope it stays that way, too." Major paused. "Where's Bask and Cato today?"

"Your brother came over yesterday and got them to help at Goodwin's sawmill for a few days."

Old Goodwin, he was really tearing things up. Chunk and Burt, too, had been working for him ever since they finished their cabin on Major's upper one hundred and sixty. "That's the first time you ever saw Lafait, huh?"

"Uh-huh."

Major waited for some comment about Lafait. They were still sitting close together on the log. He studied the cleanly curving mold of her neck and chin. Her hair was so dark there were faint blue lights in the deep waves of it. And suddenly Major was aware of the delicate scent of the woman, evoking a wild excitement in him and at the same time a great feeling of inexpressible tenderness.

She turned her face toward Major and said, "To me, it seemed that Lafait—" Her eyes widened as Major leaned forward and kissed her.

It was a gentle, almost childish, touching of their lips, and then they drew apart and stared at each other for a moment. None of the thoughts that raced through Major's mind paused long enough for understanding, and suddenly he had no desire even to try to understand them.

He stood up and drew Polly to him slowly and once more they met in a gentle, wondering kind of kiss, and then a great hot wildness surged through Major and for a time it was the same with Polly as they stood there with their arms hard around each other, blind and deaf to everything in the world but themselves.

Then Polly pushed away from Major and stepped back. She eyed him steadily, smiling. "Have you ever gone swimming in that warm pool?"

"Oh, I mud-crawled around in there some. It ain't deep enough to—to—" Major couldn't believe his eyes. Polly was unbuttoning her shirt. "Hey! What are you doing?"

Her shirt was off. "I'm going swimming, that's what I'm doing. If you don't like it, you don't have to watch."

"You—" Major mumbled, and then all he did was stare as Polly's clothes fell away under the deft movements of her hands. There she stood in her birthday suit. Her breasts were small and high, her skin faintly brown in color. A shaft of sunlight filtered through the leafy tangle and caught the dark blue tint of her hair as she turned to look at Major for an instant.

"Jeem's cousin!" he gasped.

"I don't know him," Polly said brightly. On the balls of her feet she went long-legged over the flat stones and plunged into the pool.

The breath seemed to be swelling in Major's

chest until it well nigh choked him. He didn't remember much about taking off his clothes, except that he had trouble with one boot and hopped around on the other foot until he knocked over the coffee pot, but that was no matter. The boot came off and he dropped it somewhere and ran into the warm pool.

Polly was standing waist deep in the water. She skipped her hand across the surface and jetted water into Major's face. He pawed at his eyes with one hand as he groped toward her.

"I could swim clear away from you, if this was big enough," Polly laughed.

"It ain't big enough."

He kissed her slowly, gently. She came against him with a surge and her hands were pulling at the back of his neck and he felt the swelling of her breasts against his chest.

After a time, Major lifted Polly in his arms and carried her from the pool and they went into the shelter, and that was the first of many times that they would lie together with increasing ardor in this cool, leafy place where the sunlight struck the warm pool in a broken pattern.

On that first day, and in later days, Miami Rusk scouted keenly through the parks and aspen thickets south of the secret place, suspicion in his mind and a nameless, torturing anger in his heart. He found Polly's little pony that first day, but she had left a most confusing trail, and in the end he lost it entirely.

He didn't have all the time in the world, for he was helping Lavington build up his place. It was only when Polly's father let him go hunting that he had any time to search, but even then he was rushed because he had to bring back game.

It was not every day that Polly disappeared in the hills. She had work to do at home, but she still managed to get away about three times a week. Mrs. Lavington said she had always been one to roam by herself, and so Miami figured Mrs. Lavington wasn't worried, but he was.

Miami scouted when he could for three weeks before he found Polly's pony the second time. It was with Major's horse near a spring in a down-timber thicket. A quick study of the tracks told Miami that the two animals had been left there many times.

He knew then that what he had suspected was true. It destroyed a tiny glow of brightness that had started to grow in him. Miami cursed and then he was crying and cursing savagely at the same time.

That dirty sonofabitch of a Major! Kill him!

His own promise meant something to Miami Rusk. He had given his word to Lavington that he wouldn't shoot Major, but now it was different. Lavington would thank him for what he was going to do.

So Miami lay down behind a log, put his rifle across it, and there he waited with his whole consciousness directed toward the open place where the horses were. He didn't care how long he had to wait.

As it turned out, it wasn't long at all.

The voice behind him came like the shock of a blow. "So you're going to kill him, huh, younker?"

Miami twisted around. Right off, he didn't know the tall, rough-faced man standing there as mean as the devil.

"You're going to shoot him dead, huh?"

Why, it was the old man who had come raving sick into their camp, the one Pa had unloaded on Major.

"Give me that pea shooter."

Miami leaped up. "You go to hell!"

O'Neal took the rifle away from him so quick and easy that Miami couldn't believe it had happened. He lunged to get it back and O'Neal cuffed him a lick that knocked him backward over the log. "Mind your manners," the old man said.

So dazed that the fight was temporarily knocked from him, Miami lay still for a while, thinking bitterly that this was just one more beating in the long string of them that made his life. He'd sworn that it wasn't going to happen again, but it had.

He got to his feet. O'Neal didn't say anything; he just stood there looking at him. He wasn't

93

mad, and that, Miami realized, was something very different from all other times when somebody had beat him.

This old man was as calm as swamp water.

"You ain't got reason enough to kill him," he said.

"How do you know what reason I got!"

"I know." O'Neal said it like it pained him to have to use so many words to explain something.

Sure, he probably did know everything, at that, Miami thought. Any old coot who could come through those terrible tangles of brush and timber right up to a man's back without making any noise was no ordinary man.

Staring at the dark-burned quietness of the old man, Miami suddenly knew that O'Neal was different from all other men he'd ever known. One thing, he didn't give a damn for arguments or words.

"Part Indian?" O'Neal asked.

"Yeah. Delaware."

O'Neal tossed the rifle back to Miami. "Go home."

Go back and stay with Lavingtons and have to look at Polly. Having her smile at him the same way she smiled at her brothers, while something inside was killing him. "I can't go back there!" It was almost a wail, though Miami didn't realize that.

It wasn't up to O'Neal to try to settle the woes

of the world, or even the troubles of one of its miserable inhabitants. Afterward, he'd ask himself how it happened, and the answer he gave himself always tickled him: I asked one question too many.

"Where else is there to go?" he asked.

The boy raised his head slowly. "With you."

For a long time O'Neal hadn't run into anything to surprise him, but Miami's quick words did the trick. In fact, they startled him so bad for a moment that it seemed his way of life was threatened. Take on a partner at this late stage? Him, Smith Madison O'Neal, wet nurse a skinny brat? That took the rag right off the bush, by Ephraim!

But it happened.

Miami's pleading, desperate look didn't bring it about, not by itself; O'Neal's last fever spree had a bearing in the decision. A small but solid fear had got hold of him while he was looking for his camp outfit after he recovered. He'd found his robes and possibles, though it had taken some doings. It was the insane way they were scattered around that had got to him.

He knew that if he stayed a lone wolf, the next time the fever hit him—no use bluffing himself, it was getting worse each time—he'd be off again like an Indian crazed with the pox, and maybe he wouldn't be lucky enough to fall into somebody's camp.

Going under from some kind of a scrape—knife, bullet, or the like—well, he'd been overdue for that so long that there was no fear in the thought; but to go out chewing dirt like a mad wolf after the goddamn fever had sneaked up on him just didn't set well.

Without expression he looked a moment longer at Miami. "Let's go."

The boy was all eagerness, and then he thought of something. "I'll have to tell Lavington."

O'Neal looked at the horses. He stepped forward, drawing a heavy knife so swiftly that Miami's stomach sucked in. He flipped Miami's shirt out of his belt and sliced a piece from it and thrust it at the boy. "Leave this where she'll find it."

When she started to saddle up, Polly found her bridle hanging on the tree where she had left it, with the end of one rein tied around a piece of cloth.

She recognized it at a glance, a piece from the material she and her mother had made into shirts for her brothers not a week before. Her first thought was to cry out to Major that they had been discovered. She looked around quickly, fully expecting to see her brothers somewhere close, or worse, her father.

That quick panic didn't hold for long; she was not the kind to enlarge her own fears. If her brothers were nearby, spying, they would not have left a warning. That's what it was, a warning that they knew about her and Major. Beyond that, she didn't care to guess.

She looked at Major, who was almost ready to leave. Why didn't he say that this sneaking around was no good? Why didn't he ask her to go home with him? Why hadn't he mentioned one single word about marriage? She glanced at the cloth in her fist.

"Hey, you'd better hurry up, Polly."

She put the cloth into her shirt pocket.

Major came over and picked up her saddle and set it on the pony. "What are you moping about?"

"Nothing. I can do that saddling." She reached under the pony and grabbed the swinging cinch. "You'd better get along, Major."

"Maybe I ought to. I've got some chores to do." Major went back to Smoke. "When can you get away again?"

Get away. Yes, that was how a man would put it. "I don't know," Polly said. "It may be quite a while."

"You're right." Major nodded thoughtfully. "We'd best be a little more careful about coming here too often."

"You go on out, Major. I'll be along in a minute."

He hesitated. "Do you feel all right? I mean—"

"I'm all right. Go ahead."

Major lead his horse away. For several minutes Polly stood beside her pony, thinking about her behavior, and then, without regret or guilt, she went home to face whatever was waiting there.

Mrs. Lavington was in an irritable mood. "I'm getting weary of your eternal kiting around in the mountains, Polly. Considering the way things are going—"

"Where's Pa and the boys?"

Mrs. Lavington sighed. "A committee meeting at the Stenhouse place. They're planning more trouble, I know. As if we didn't have enough grief just getting here in the first place, without them fixing to tear the country apart. I can understand your pa's feelings, but when he drags the boys—"

"Did they wear their new shirts?"

"Their new shirts? What's that got to do with what I'm saying?"

"Did they?"

"No! I gave Bask's shirt to Miami, anyway. It's a wonder your pa didn't take him along too."

"Miami. Oh, I see now."

"You see what? What are you talking about anyway, Polly?"

Polly showed her mother the piece of shirt. "Miami left this hanging where he knew I'd be sure to find it."

"It's the material, sure enough. Maybe he accidentally tore his shirt and—"

"No! He left it as some kind of message, I know."

Mrs. Lavington fingered the cloth. She studied her daughter closely. "That boy has had calf eyes for you ever since he came here. Some younguns that age are as rutty as goats. Have you stirred him up—? Oh, I know you wouldn't mean anything by it, but if—"

"I've got eyes, Ma," Polly said. "I've never done anything but treat him decent."

Mrs. Lavington sighed. "With a boy like that, sometimes you don't have to do anything at all. Their insides are out of whack."

"I don't think he's coming back," Polly said. "I think that's what he was trying to tell us by leaving the piece of shirt."

When, an hour after dark, Miami had not returned, Mrs. Lavington was inclined to agree with her daughter. "I don't understand, though, why he did it all of a sudden." She eyed Polly thoughtfully.

Chapter Eight

Coming home after a week at cow camp, Toby McAllister saw the new cabin across the creek. Five or six kids were milling around in the yard and a huge woman was yelling orders at a little man.

Hell in a pigpen! The cabin was smack in the middle of McAllister winter pasture. Toby's heavy-boned face was white with anger as he galloped downriver to his father's place. He found old Shad digging postholes for a new corral.

"Where the hell have you been?" Toby yelled, even before he dismounted. "There's a new claim shack a mile up the river!"

Old Shad rammed his bar into the posthole and wiped his brow with his sleeve. "So it's started."

"What's started?" Toby demanded.

"We had a rumor last week that the Regulators were going to settle people on unified ground. Lavington called a meeting at Big Harve's place and—"

"To hell with that! Let's go chase those people off our land right now!"

They went directly to the cabin. The man, a little fellow with bushy, ginger colored whiskers, was laying green slabs on the pole roof.

"Look at that!" Toby growled. "Goodwin has got his sawmill going, and the first thing he's done is to use it to help people like them."

"Who are you fellers?" the man on the roof asked.

"McAllisters," Shad said. "You're on our land."

The little man sat down on the roof. "Name's York, Jeremy B. York, from Ioway. Glad to know you fellers. I heard about you."

"Then you ought to know you're on the wrong piece of land," Toby said.

"Sure enough, you must be funning. Did you hear that, Birdie?" York shouted down to his huge wife.

"Sure enough," Birdie said. The kids were clustered hard around her.

"You folks better git right now!" Toby yelled.

"You hear that, Birdie?"

"I sure do."

Toby reached for the rifle in his saddle boot. Old Shad knocked his arm down. "Look at those kids, you idiot."

"They say this ain't your land," York said mildly. "I ain't aiming to move, unless somebody proves I made a mistake."

"You're going to move now!" Toby shouted.

"That's easy to say, mister, but you don't know the trouble I have just getting Birdie in the wagon. Now there's a sure enough chore for you."

"Get down from that roof," Toby ordered.

"No thank you."

"Maybe a bullet will change your mind!"

"If the Lord says it's my time to be shot, then I guess I'll just have to be shot," York said mildly.

Toby dismounted. "You get their team, Pa."

Mrs. York sat down on the ground. Her children gathered around her. Toby tried to lift her and discovered that it was sure enough a big chore. She offered him nothing but dead weight. The children kicked his shins. A girl snatched his pistol from the holster and dropped it, and one of her small brothers kicked him as he bent to pick it up.

"Pa!" Toby bawled. "Give me a hand!"

Pa stayed on his horse. His son, who could break beaver dams, build miles of fences, and wrestle steers to the ground, found himself defeated by a fat woman and her brood. Toby limped away from the frustrating task and waved his fist at York.

"You tell her to get up!"

York shook his head sadly. "Only the Lord can move her."

"I can move you!" Toby bellowed. He ran to the makeshift ladder leaning against the logs. The second rung broke under his great weight and his knee scraped hard against the rough crosspiece above it. He untangled himself and lurched away, rubbing his leg.

"I made that ladder just to hold me," York explained. "You're a pretty big man, McAllister."

Toby drew his pistol. "Get down from there, York!"

The little man shook his head. "Go ahead and shoot. That'll leave Birdie a widow with six kids, but maybe the Lord will take care of them better than I been able to. Yes, sir, you just go right ahead and shoot me."

Baffled, Toby looked to his father for help. Old Shad shook his head.

And then Fred Grosland stepped out from the trees up the hill with a rifle in his hands. "That's enough! Put the six-shooter away, Toby, or try to use it."

Toby was mad enough to make the try. He hesitated, sizing up the chances, and then he saw the glint of two more rifles in the trees. He put his pistol away.

"That's being smart," Grosland said. "I guess you know my boys have got claims below here. You try to give them any trouble and you're going to run into it just like you did here." He shifted the rifle around. "Now you McAllisters git!"

"We'll be back," Toby promised.

"Bring plenty of help, because you're going to find plenty of us," Grosland said.

It pleased Bill Gifford to bring word to the Pilchers that four claims had been staked on their land by a family named Shepler.

Gifford was a trimly built man with dark hair, an infectious smile, and clear gray eyes that could lie as easily as his full lips.

Luke Pilcher cursed mightily. "I seen that wagonload when they passed here. Twice, by God! They'd been to Goodwin's. Now there's a sonofabitch we ought to—"

"They're a hard bunch," Gifford said.

"The Regulators put 'em up to it," Matt said. "So they think they can start on us, huh?"

"It's not just you boys," Gifford said.

"Lavington's kids have taken up Tad Sherman's lower meadows."

"To hell with old wishy-washy Sherman," Mark Pilcher growled. "He's like Major Whitlock. How come nobody's bothered him?"

No one said anything for a while, and then Matt said, "Lafait is no bigger than one bullet."

"Old Maje," Luke said, "he's the one who gave the Regulators the idea of putting people on claims he's been hogging. If he hadn't started the idea—"

Matt cursed. "What are we arguing about Lafait and Major for? Let's get up there where them squatters are. Damn it all anyway, they wouldn't have got settled if Mark and Luke had been riding that country the way I said."

"Now don't be blaming your brothers, Matt," Ross said. "We've all been—"

"Aw, shut up, Pa," Matt growled. "Let's go."

Gifford went with them. At the first cabin they found evidence that someone had just left, and it was the same at the next two. Mark put his rope around the ends of two logs at the corner of the third cabin and set his horse to pull the place apart. The heavy green logs were too much. The rope broke and Mark sat there on his horse cursing.

"That was a fool stunt in the first place," Matt said. "Let's get on up to their main hangout."

They did that, all in a bunch, with great purpose and no plan. That approach had worked very well before on others who had tried to settle on

Pilcher ground. About all the tribe had had to do was to arrive on the scene, bristling with scowls, firearms, and threats.

It tickled Gifford to see the forthright way the Pilchers went in on the Shepler headquarters. It also made him nervous.

Old man Shepler was a stocky fellow with a sandy spade beard, a big chaw of tobacco and a shotgun, which he held cocked as he stood in the doorway of a half completed cabin. His wife was standing behind him with a dishpan full of pistols, a gaunt woman puffing a short clay pipe.

From three places in the brush around the cabin burly young Sheplers watched with hard eyes and rifles.

It was not an inviting situation, as the Pilchers agreed afterward.

Matt did the talking, considerable of it, to all of which old man Shepler listened quietly without changing expression. After Matt had his say, Shepler spat a stream of tobacco juice into the bright chips in the yard. "Get off our land."

There wasn't much else to do.

"This ain't the last of it!" Mark yelled.

All the way down the river the Pilchers cursed each other for doing things wrong. They should have surrounded the place. They should have caught the sons one at a time at the lower cabins. They should have gone in on foot, shooting. They should have done a lot of things differently.

At the last cabin downriver, Luke dismounted. "By God, I'll burn this one anyway!"

Old Ross shook his head. "Them logs? Fat chance."

Luke and Mark gave it a try anyway, piling brush and chips and limbs against the side of the cabin. Their fire merely charred the exterior of the cabin logs. "Everybody get more wood!" Luke shouted.

"Forget it," Ross said disgustedly.

Matt knocked down part of the mud and stone fireplace chimney and Mark broke some cast iron cooking utensils he found inside, and with that the Pilchers resumed their quarreling way toward home.

"What are we going to do, boys?" Gifford asked.

Matt said, "We? Nobody has settled on your land."

"If the Sheplers get away with this, you can bet someone will move up my way before long. It seems to me that this thing is a problem for every honest man in the country."

"That's right," Ross said. "We're going straight down to Burnine's this very minute. No sense in one family trying to fight this thing alone." It was the first show of authority he had made in a long time.

"Major and Lafait ought to be in on it," Gifford said.

"That Major thinks he can stay clear by hiring

people to stay on his land," Matt said angrily, "but that don't go down with me. Either he's with us or he's on the other side, and by God, I want to hear him say it one way or the other today!"

"I guess we can stop at his place on the way down." Gifford was well pleased. He was never so happy as when fomenting trouble, especially if he could direct his efforts against Major Whitlock.

In the middle of the afternoon Lafait delivered the load of lumber to Major, hauling it in the rickety Whitlock wagon drawn by Fawn and Steuben. "How the hell did we ever come all the way from Kentucky with oxen?"

"We made it," Major said. "Slow. But we made it."

"I haven't got time to help you unload. I'm headed for Denver to pick up a new wagon for Goodwin, and I'm going to get him a team of mules that can move."

Lafait had caught his horse and saddled up before he thought to give his brother more news. "Things are kind of stirred up down south. Your Regulators are settled in seven or eight places that the old timers claim." Lafait grinned. "The Groslands are telling a funny story about how Toby McAllister tried to pick up a fat woman, and her kids pummelled the daylights out of him."

"I don't follow you. What fat woman—"

"You'll hear about it." Lafait mounted his horse. He hesitated. "You'll be all right here, won't you?"

"Sure. Why not?"

Lafait shrugged. "You're legal, I guess. Maybe a little hoggish, but legal."

"Now look here, Lafait—"

"See you in a week or thereabouts." Lafait grinned and rode away at a fast trot.

Major looked at the stack of green lumber. Now he was that much more in debt, and it was going to take at least two more loads of lumber to do what he had in mind. First, he was going to build a storeroom to get rid of some of the plunder crowding the cabin. Then he was going to put a floor in the cabin.

After that, he figured on building a kitchen and a bedroom. And then, if he lost his mind entirely, he was going to buy a cookstove.

The lumber was here, and he had a keg of square nails, and he had figured out on paper just how he wanted to build the storeroom.

He had sawed enough boards for the back wall of the storehouse when Toby McAllister arrived.

Toby had something on his mind and was in no mood for small talk. "We're going to meet at our place tonight."

That was the McAllister way, just bow the neck and bull headlong into things, and Major had got more or less used to it, but today his brother-in-law's approach struck him all wrong, him just barreling up like that and the same as ordering Major to come to a meeting.

Major tried to keep calm. "How's Dorcas and the boy?"

"If you ever came by you'd know."

Major took a deep breath. "What's the matter, Toby?"

"All hell's broke loose. The Groslands and some other worthless bunch are on our land, and there's squatters all over the flats west of Burnine. We're going to settle things this time, and we don't want you bollixing up the deal."

Major bristled. "Who's *we?*"

"All of us. We're fed up with you sticking up for your friend Lavington, and other trash like the Rusks. I hear you even took in the oldest Rusk brat."

"That ain't quite the straight of it," Major said slowly. He was holding a hand saw. He sighted down the back of it while he waited for Toby to ask a question, but Toby was in no mood to ask for explanations.

He just sat there in the saddle all mad and worried, with sweat soaking down from his high, strong neck, and the whole powerful, raw-boned tenseness of him said he was fairly spoiling for a fight.

Well, he wasn't going to get it from Major.

"Climb down, Toby, and set a minute and we'll talk about what's bothering you."

"I ain't got time. I'm on my way to see the Pilchers, that is, if there's any left that you haven't talked into running away from home." Toby started to turn his horse.

"Now just a minute. That's another thing that you ain't quite got the straight of." Major put the saw down and walked over to the horse. "There's no reason for you and me to quarrel. If you'd—"

"Be at the meeting. That's all I got to say." Toby started away.

"I won't be there," Major called after him.

Toby checked his horse and came back. "Do you know what you're saying?"

"I won't be at your damned meeting, or any other miserable get-together where you talk about hanging men. Acting like a bunch of sneaking bushwhackers ain't my idea of a way to do anything."

"Oh, no! Your idea is to hire folks to hold down your land, and that's about as sneaky as you can get. You sit here in your stinking little valley like a lord of creation, living off your step-father and backed up by that murdering brother of yours—"

"Keep your tongue off Lafait."

"Why? Because you're hiding behind him? Because he's a cold blooded killer? If you think—"

Major dragged him out of the saddle then. With a grunt and a curse Toby came down across Major's shoulder as the horse sidestepped away, snorting. Major's knees buckled, but he bent his back and took the full weight, and then he got his hands up and around Toby's neck and unloaded him in a bone-jarring, twisting roll through the cut ends of boards.

Toby came up with hell in his eyes. He was wearing a pistol but he forgot all about it. He hunched his shoulders and came in windmilling his arms. Major crouched and met him belly high with a driving shoulder and sent him sprawling again.

No McAllister was known for quitting. Toby was awkward but he was horse-strong and eager. He came in flailing like a man trying to beat a fence post into the ground with his bare hands. The side of his wrist raked down Major's face and peeled his nose and a broken button on his cuff ripped a gash in Major's cheek that left a scar for life.

Major tried to grapple with him. He might as well have tried to stop a log rolling downhill. Toby knocked his hands away and sent him reeling backward into a board lying across two saw-horses. The board broke and dropped Major on his hind-sides between the shattered ends. For an instant Major thought that maybe Toby was going to let the scuffle end right there, for he hesitated.

"I'm willing to—" Major said, and then he back-scuttled desperately on his hands and heels. Toby had taken one driving step and was in the air, trying to come down on Major with his knees and elbows.

As he got in the clear, Major ripped the heel of

his hand on the teeth of the saw lying on the ground. Once more Toby was hesitating, crouched on his hands and knees, staring at Major. He was not thinking of quitting, Major realized; he never would quit.

He was too much for a skull and knuckle fight. Major reached back to grasp the saw. He didn't find it right away and so he took a quick glance round. He saw something better, Toby's pistol lying in the dirt and sawdust. Major grabbed the weapon and leaped up.

"That's enough, Toby!"

The weapon made no difference to Toby. He rose, lowered his head and hunched his shoulders and charged. Major sidestepped, tripping him as he lunged past. Toby fell over a stack of boards and hit the ground with a sodden impact that seemed more than enough to knock the breath out of him and sense into him.

The fall had no effect, except to make him hesitate a little longer than usual after he got up. If he had talked, shouted, or cursed—anything—Major would have felt better, but Toby only stared with that same look of blankness. He set himself for another rush.

"Stop it!" Major fired the pistol into the air.

Toby came at him again.

Once more Major sidestepped and this time he took a full arm swing with the pistol against the side of Toby's head. His rush carried him on for several wobbling steps, and then he turned to come back. Blood ran down past his ear. His mouth was open. He stared at Major and tried to gather himself to rush again, and then he fell headlong on his face.

Major was still afraid of him. He walked over slowly and bent above him. Horror gripped Major then. He saw brain matter mixed with the blood on the side of Toby's head. Oh Christ, I've killed him! He wanted to cry out to someone that he had not wanted this to happen, that he had tried his best not to harm Toby McAllister.

Never again in his life would Major get the reprieve which came to him then. Toby groaned and tried to raise his head, and Major saw that what he had thought was brain matter was only leaf mold and dirt and bloody sawdust.

"Lay still, Toby, just lay still!" Major ran to the spring and got water in the rusty tin can dipper and came trotting back with it. Toby was sitting up, grunting in pain as he held his left shoulder.

Blood dripping from his scalp wound fell on his hand and made him think that he had a bullet in the shoulder. "You've ruined my whole arm," he muttered dazedly.

"That blood is coming from your hard head." Major poured water over the cut. Toby kept insisting that he was shot in the shoulder. He had hurt it one of those times when he thumped into the ground, Major thought, but even after he removed

Toby's shirt, the injured man took several minutes before he was convinced that he had no bullet hole in him.

"You damn fool," Major said, "what's the idea of coming in here, starting a fight and going hog wild? You were set to kill me and I couldn't even make you hear me." He picked up his saw. It was bent.

"When I get real mad, I lose my head," Toby said slowly.

"I believe that." Major bowed the saw, trying to take the bend out of it. He sighted down the back. Hell, it was kinked.

"You've got blood all over your face, Major."

"I guess it'll wash off."

Toby looked about half sick. He sat down on a sawhorse, holding his wadded shirt against his head. "We've been worried about things, and now they've started to happen. We was sore at you, Major, because you didn't want to stick with us. All the way up here I was boiling about things in general."

Toby got up and went over to his horse. He took the shirt away from his head and felt the cut with the tips of his fingers. "It's quit bleeding, I reckon. You know, I'm going to feel pretty sheepish when Dorcas starts asking questions and I have to tell her that you and me was fighting."

"Somebody will have worse questions than that to answer, if you all keep listening to Burnine."

Toby shook his shirt out and began to put it on, grimacing at the pain in his shoulder. "What do *you* say we ought to do?"

Major had no answer. He knew what he was going to do and that was as far as he cared to think.

Toby got his shirt on. "I've still got to go to Pilcher Town, so—"

"No, you don't," Major said, looking across the meadow. "Here they come." And Bill Gifford with them.

Matt, Mark, and Luke all tried to talk at the same time after they dismounted. They were trying to tell Toby what had happened up their way and he was trying to get in a word about events down on Little Creek. Major was surprised to hear old Ross cut the whole bunch off and tell about the Sheplers himself.

"That's only half of it," Toby said. He told the Pilchers and Gifford about what had happened down on Little Creek.

Major sat on a sawhorse and wished the whole gabbling outfit would leave.

"What do you think now, Major?" Gifford asked. "Are you ready to go with us?"

Oh, he seemed real concerned about it, Gifford did, but Major knew the question was aimed at stirring up trouble. Gifford knew damn well how Major felt.

Major didn't even bother to look at Gifford. The

Apostles walked over and Matt said, "He asked you something, Maje."

"So he did." From the corner of his eye Major saw Mark ease around to the left. Luke shifted to the other side. Now they had Major hemmed in.

Old Ross saw the drift of things. "All right, boys. We didn't stop here to—"

"Shut up, Pa," Matt said. He looked at Major. "Yeah, we want you to answer that question."

"I'll take care of this here valley," Major said, "without help from the Pilchers or anyone else."

Matt grinned. "Now that takes the lid off the kraut barrel." He glanced at his brothers. "Ain't that something, boys?"

Old Ross tried again. "Just a minute here! I—"

Matt glanced over his shoulder. He turned just enough to put his hand against his father's chest and push Ross away violently. "I let you run things for an hour or so, and that's enough."

No one was going to interfere, Major knew. He'd half expected Toby to make at least some protest against what was coming, but Toby seemed to be confused, scowling and staring and unable to make up his mind. Old Ross was beat; his sons had overwhelmed him long before. And Gifford, he couldn't keep the sneaky look of enjoyment out of his expression.

Let it be so. Major didn't want any help. The Pilchers would hammer him down, he didn't doubt, but he would leave a mark here and there before it was over. He didn't move from the sawhorse, but he drew his feet back and got them firmly set.

Standing about five feet away, in front of Major, Matt said, "So you don't need no help with your valley, huh, Maje? All you have to do is talk half-grown idiots like Chunk and Burt into running away from home to help you. For a man that looks like he's been beat up good once already today, you sure got a big, loose mouth."

Matt had to build up to it with words and insults. That was the Pilcher way.

It was not Major's way. When Matt started talking again, Major moved. He didn't take his weight any higher than necessary, just high enough to get off the sawhorse. Mark reacted quicker than the others, as Major had figured he would. "Watch him!" he yelled, and tried to rush in to slug Major before he was on his feet.

Major sent the sawhorse skidding toward Mark and in the same motion drove forward in a crouch to sink his shoulder into Matt's belly. The sawhorse took Mark across the knees. He went over it and fell hard, plunging one hand into the keg of nails.

Matt was caught by surprise. Major hit him where he was aiming but his foot had slipped on a board scrap and his drive lost much of its power. As it was, he knocked Matt back into old Ross. Ross went down with a surprised grunt but the impact saved Matt from falling. While he was off balance Major cracked three of his ribs with a sweeping blow.

That was the last advantage Major won. He spun around in time to dump Luke over his shoulder by ducking low as Luke charged in wildly. Then Mark, blood flying from the hand he had jammed into the nails, caught Major on the temple with a hard blow. Major went down and nothing was very clear after that. He remembered getting up one time with a broken board in his hands.

He couldn't find an Apostle to strike but Gifford's face appeared hazily and so he hit Gifford over the head with the piece of lumber. The Apostles came in on all sides, working Major over thoroughly. When he couldn't rise, they began to kick him.

They didn't finish him, not quite. He grappled with a leg that was as stout as a post, trying to spill the man standing over him. He seemed to be putting tremendous strength into the effort, but the leg didn't move, and at last Major slid back on the ground and lay there, dully aware.

It was Toby McAllister standing over him. Toby was cursing the Pilchers as cowardly bastards, one arm hanging useless, his eyes wild.

The Apostles fell back from him, looking at him uneasily.

"Get out of here!" Toby shouted.

"I guess he's had enough, at that," Matt

muttered. "Come on, boys." When they were mounted, he said to Toby, "You mean you're throwing in with him?"

"Get out!"

The Pilchers and Gifford rode away. Only Gifford had any understanding of what had happened. It was merely that some men believed in fair play, which to Gifford was a rather simple-minded philosophy. Fair play was all right, if you could afford it for appearances' sake, but it had no merit as a guide in life if it was going to cost too much.

"That Toby went crazy!" Matt complained. His ribs were giving him hell. "We should have stomped him down with Major."

"If you'd hurt him just a little, I think he would have gone crazy," Gifford said shrewdly. "I've seen men like him before. You have to kill them to stop them."

"We can do that, if we have to," Mark said. He had torn and ripped his right hand brutally, and he was trying not to think of blood poisoning. One nail had been driven clear through his hand.

"Don't worry about Toby," Gifford said. "He'll be along."

He was quite right. Toby had jumped in to prevent Major from being crippled or killed, and now, with Major on his feet, Toby was ready to go. No matter what else the Pilchers were, they were still his allies.

It had been a miserable day. On the second try he managed to get on his horse. Pain made his heavy features ugly as he tried to get his left arm into a comfortable position. He looked at Major and tried to think of a way to express his feelings. "Well, hell," he said at last, and rode away to catch up with the Pilchers.

Major lay down in the cool shade near the spring. He knew now why Lafait had said that it was silly to fight skull and knuckle; if you wanted to hurt a man, do it right: kill him with a pistol.

He rolled over painfully and reached for the tin can dipper on the rock beside the spring.

Drinking, Major slopped water unsteadily. It ran down his chin and on his chest and it felt so good that he took another dipperful and doused himself before lying back with a sigh.

He was dozing lightly sometime later when he was roused by Polly's voice calling from near the cabin. He answered and tried to get up, but he couldn't make it until he got hold of a tree and hauled himself to his feet.

She came swiftly through the trees. Shock struck her face like a blow when she saw Major. "It ain't that bad," he said.

"It's awful, Major. What—what on earth happened?"

She was beautiful standing there with her eyes wide, like a young doe motionless for a moment in leaf-broken sunlight. In spite of his hurts and aches Major wanted her fiercely. The force of his feeling under the circumstances puzzled him and made him feel half ashamed. "I had a few words with the Apostles."

"Are you all right?"

"Sure!"

"No, you're not. You look like fresh beef."

Suddenly Major grinned. "I feel that way, too." He made no protest when Polly led him into the cabin.

"Who cut your face with the knife?"

"No one had a knife. Jeem's cousin! What are you trying to do, pull my whole cheek apart?"

"You've got dirt in that cut. I'm going to clean it out and then I'm going to sew it up, or else you'll look like a whopper-jawed mule." She did the job with a common needle and white cotton thread, twenty-seven stitches from Major's cheekbone to the middle of his lower jaw.

It seemed to Major that there were a hundred knotted thread ends when he felt the repair afterward, and though he joked with Polly about her over-doing the needlework at the time, he was grateful afterward, for the cut healed cleanly, leaving only a thin scar line.

"Old Toby must have caught me with a finger-nail, or something."

"Toby McAllister? Was he in on it?"

Major wished he'd kept his mouth shut. "Naw,

that was a separate scuffle. We're not mad at each other."

"You had a real busy day, didn't you?" Polly put him in a chair and told him to stay there. "I'll make some coffee." She frowned at the fireplace. It was hotter than Tophet in the cabin and her face was shining with sweat. "Outside."

Major sat on a stool in the shade while she boiled coffee over a small fire. He watched her with pleasure, and occasionally when she glanced at him and caught his eyes on her, she gave him a little smile with the teasing quirk in it. He kept rolling around the idea that maybe now was a good time to tell her about flooring the cabin and about the room he had in mind to add, with a cookstove. Come to think of it, a damn fireplace *was* sort of unhandy for cooking.

Though Major knew the way to get at the thing he had in mind was just to up and say, "Polly, let's get married," it wasn't so danged easy to blurt out. Not that he was scared. Cautious was more like it. "You know, Polly, I'm pretty bad in debt, and there's a lot of trouble brewing, but still I've been wondering if maybe—"

The snap of brush somewhere in the trees stopped him.

"Yes?" Polly said.

Major raised a cautioning hand. A few moments later he saw O'Neal and Miami coming through the grove on foot. Miami was leading O'Neal's horse, which was laden with deer meat slung in a fresh hide. Without pausing Miami veered away from the spring and led the horse on to the cabin before he stopped. And there he stood with his back turned, defiant and quite apart from the others and making sure that they could see his attitude.

Hard shaved as usual, with his ragged gray hair spilling wildly from under an old hat, O'Neal came straight on to the spring. He looked Major over and said, "We seen the Pilchers riding south. They looked sort of used. I figured something might have happened here. Anything to be done about it?"

Major tried to grin. It felt like he was tearing all the stitches out of his cheek. "No. Everything's all right."

"That's good. Then I'll just leave you two some meat and go on." O'Neal glanced at Polly. He did not raise his voice when he said, "Miami, leave a haunch there in the cabin."

Major observed how quickly the boy moved, though he kept his back to the spring as much as possible. O'Neal declined to stay for coffee. "Trouble or not, I'll be around the cabin for a spell." He went over to where Miami was tying the hide up again, and then the two of them walked off.

They were an odd pair, for sure, Major thought, but it looked like Miami had at last found somebody he respected.

Polly threw her coffee away. "He knows about us."

"Huh! How do you know?"

"I could tell by the one look he gave me. Miami knows too. That's why he never went back to our place."

"O'Neal won't say anything, and I'll bet he sees that Miami don't either."

"That's comforting," Polly said sharply. "Is that your only comment?"

Puzzled by the sudden coldness in her expression, Major didn't know what to say.

"I've got to go home."

"What's the big hurry?"

Polly picked up the coffee pot and stamped the fire out with her foot. "Bask and Cato have had a little trouble with Mr. Sherman, and Ma's worried and so I don't want to leave her alone too long."

It sounded like a pretty flimsy excuse to Major, but in view of Polly's bitey mood, he didn't want to start a quarrel by saying so. "What happened with Sherman?"

"Bask and Cato took up his lower meadows."

"My God!"

Polly flared back at him. "It was open ground!"

"Well, yeah, I know, but—"

"But what?"

"He said there was room for everybody. I didn't think—"

"Well, he's changed his mind now."

That was natural, Major thought; it was pretty easy to forgive other people's enemies; but when they became your enemies, that was different.

Polly started toward the cabin with the pot and the cups, and then she stopped and put them down on the ground. "I guess you ain't so feeble but what you can lift these." She walked off in the trees to get her pony.

Major hobbled after her. "I don't know what I said that made you so mad, Polly."

She rode away while Major was still protesting.

Chapter Nine

The meeting at Shad McAllister's place threatened to break up in angry discord almost as soon as it began. Carl Burnine said the whole mess had come about because the others had been too spineless to hang Lavington when Burnine first suggested it. "It's not too late yet. Let's go do it now."

"That won't get the Yorks and the Groslands off our land!" Jake McAllister yelled.

"We can hang them later," Burnine growled.

After a violent argument, Burnine gave in. The majority was for cleaning out all the interlopers in the Little Creek area. Later, they would deal with the others one by one.

Eben and Uriah Martin were not present.

Burnine had sent a messenger to their place, but the brothers' wives had said their husbands were out hunting and they did not know when they would return.

No matter, Burnine said. They had thirteen men, counting his foreman, Frank Jordan, and three other Burnine riders who were waiting now for orders.

Matt Pilcher suggested that they divide into three groups and hit three places at the same time.

"No," Burnine said curtly. "We'll be a striking force only if we all stay together. You can damn well figure we're going to have trouble with the Groslands, so we'd better be in one bunch."

At early dark they rode to Joe Bob Stenhouse's claim. Joe Bob was not home. The cabin walls were of logs, but the roof was made of lumber from Goodwin's mill. In the yard was a wagon Joe Bob had borrowed from his father.

Frank Jordan made a swift appraisal of the place. "Mr. Burnine, if we load up his woodpile in that wagon, run it up against the wall, and have about five men put ropes on the front end of the rafters and get the horses to pull at the same time . . ." Jordan seemed to know what he was talking about.

Under his direction they wrecked the cabin and set the wreckage on fire.

Matt Pilcher, who could not do any work because of his ribs, began to worry about the fire being seen.

"You'd have to be up in the hills to see it," Jake McAllister said. "There's too many trees between here and Grosland's for them to see it."

"And those green logs will never burn enough to light up the sky," Jordan added. "I remember down in Georgia when we were burning—" He let it drop.

Burnine knew that his foreman had been in the Yankee army, but this was the first he'd heard him say anything about Georgia. *Burning, eh?* With Sherman on the way to Savannah, sure as hell. The war was over, but there was one part of it that still lay like a festering sliver in Burnine's mind.

Frank Jordan was a good man with cattle, and a good foreman. Tomorrow Burnine would fire him. Clem Pettigrew, a Texan who had been with Hood, could have the job.

Success with the first cabin created a contagion of excitement that sheer destruction always brings.

"Let's get the rest of them!" Luke Pilcher yelled.

As the raiders started away, two oxen lumbered up, their broad faces turned toward the fire. Mark Pilcher shot the nearest one with his pistol. The animal went down on its forelegs and its eyes held a mildly puzzled look.

"There was no call for that!" Shad McAllister yelled.

Mark laughed. "They got no wagon to hitch it to."

He raised his pistol to shoot the second ox.

"That's enough shooting!" Burnine said crisply.

They rode down to Burnine's place and stopped briefly in the yard to make their plans for the strike against the Groslands. "We're bound to get scattered a little," Burnine said. "The password will be 'Shiloh'."

From a dark upstairs window, Susan Burnine looked down on the shadowy figures in the yard. From her other window, in the gable, she had seen the fire, and now, listening to the talk below, she found the whole scene frightening and unreal. Those men down there couldn't be the same ones she knew by daylight.

They were laughing and joking about the destruction they had done, and about what they were going to do before the night was over. And Jake McAllister . . . Why, he was the biggest savage of them all. Her parents were urging her to marry him, now that she had refused to go to school in Virginia. Marry him? That thought seemed as unreal as the activity in the yard below.

Now they were getting ready to leave. She heard Matt Pilcher curse bitterly as he struggled into the saddle. She heard her father say, "Let's understand each other, boys. This won't be easy but we're going through with it, no matter what kind of fight they put up. Do we understand that?"

"By God, every man here had better understand it," Jake said. "I'm for shooting anybody that even talks about backing out."

His words carried a tone of unnecessary anger. They caused an awkward silence.

"I've got a big-mouthed son," Old Shad growled. Now I'll say something to you all. We'll do what seems necessary but if there's any hanging talk, you'd better put the rope on me first. Is that understood too?"

There was a short silence. A horse blew and stamped.

"Since you're aiming at me, Shad," Burnine said quietly, "I'll answer that. No one gets hanged—tonight."

They rode away into the heavy gloom of the surrounding trees. Susan went back to her bed after a time, lying there unsleeping. Suddenly she wished that Major Whitlock was with the raiders, and that he was riding to get himself killed by one of the Groslands.

And then she turned her face into the pillow and cried.

Three people besides the raiders had seen the flames of Joe Bob's ruined cabin.

Returning late from prowling the mountains, Uriah and Eben Martin had been told by their wives about the meeting at McAllister's. It was too late then for them to make the meeting, and anyway they had seen enough of jawbone sessions that produced no killing.

This evening they ate supper together in Eben's

cabin, where his wife, Alethea, had cooked a pot of black-eyed peas. Fiona, Uriah's spouse, had come from the adjoining cabin, and the two women sat silently in the shadows away from the table while their husbands ate.

The women were sisters, once passing fair of face and form during their girlhood days in Franklin County, Missouri. Alethea and Fiona had married the Martin brothers in a double ceremony, much to the disgust of sober citizens who declared that the Martin boys had been nothing but low-down bushwhackers most of their lives.

This basic fact was true, and it had not been changed by the Martins' moving farther west.

The women were changed, however. Now they were sallow and snaggle-toothed. Their thinning hair was drawn back tightly and held in a bun. They wore ragged dresses that brushed the dirt floor where their bare feet rested.

Midway in the meal Uriah said, "Maybe those nabobs have decided to do something, brother Eben. We'd best have a look, don't you think?"

Eben thought it over and nodded with a grin. "They just might have got around to something."

Disorder, fear, strife always did something for the brothers' souls. Years of bushwhacking had taught them that careful men could always move profitably on the edge of trouble.

Even without profit, there were other rewards. Killing was a narcotic that soothed the mind. So far, Uriah had held Eben back. Killing Burnine's dogs and shooting three of Major Whitlock's steers had been some release, but Eben longed for bigger game.

Nudged by Alethea, Fiona at last got up courage to say, "We heerd there was a doctor in the country now."

Always whining about their aching teeth, Uriah thought. "We'll bring him up if we run across him," he said. It was the same answer he had given for years. Hell, teeth fell out naturally enough, with no need of a fancy doctor.

The Martins hurried through the rest of their meal and rode away, past the barn where six thousand in gold was buried.

From the break of the hill downriver, they saw the fire at Joe Bob's cabin.

"By God, they did start something!" Flames in the night always excited Eben.

"We'll set a spell and figure out what to do," Uriah said.

Other than the raiders, Ernst Grosland was the third man to see the burning cabin. He was coming in from hunting, with two deer on a packhorse, and he was high enough to have a full view of the valley.

He left the packhorse to come in by itself and made a wild ride through the pinons to his brother's claim shack, where he found William already in bed.

"You go down and warn Pa," Ernst said. "I'll go tell Jeremy York. Then we'll all come back here, just like we've planned."

Ernst's place was made of boards. The Groslands had figured to sacrifice it in case of trouble. William's house was made of green logs, and the Groslands had taken certain measures to make it a strong point.

Ernst rode away while his brother was dressing. The Yorks were all gathered at their hewed log table and the father was reading to them from the Bible by the dim light of a coal oil lantern.

Jeremy York was not impressed by Ernst's story.

"The Lord will take care of us," he said.

The children nodded and said, "Amen!"

Ernst cursed in German, apologized, and tried to talk the Yorks into leaving while there was time.

"We are on our own land," Jeremy said, "and the Lord—"

"Suit yourself, York," Ernst said, "but if you get burned out, don't say we didn't warn you."

"You saw a fire. That don't prove much, does it?" York asked.

"We don't know, but we ain't taking any chances. We know they're going to come sooner or later. Pa says Burnine is the kind who can't wait too long to do something, so—"

"So you're going to fight back with the same kind of force they use," York said.

"Hell yes!" Ernst cried. "We'll show 'em how

the boar et the cabbage if they come fooling around."

York refused to budge. He restated his faith in a higher power than bullets.

"We always figured to lose my place in case of a raid," Ernst said, "and if you don't want to fight for yours, you'll lose it whether you stay or not, but we plan to make it cost them so high to tackle William's cabin that they won't come back a second time."

"Blood is not the answer," York said firmly.

"It's our answer." Ernst argued no more.

In the dark the raiders missed the easy crossing of Little Creek and got into an area where the McAllisters had broken beaver dams. Shad's horse put a foreleg into a deep pocket of silt with a buried tangle of sticks and aspen logs. In a hard lunge to free itself, the animal broke its leg.

They got the horse out and Shad stripped the gear from it. Before anyone knew what he intended to do, he drew his pistol and shot the animal, and then he said bitterly, "That was the best goddamn horse I ever had."

He went on foot from then on.

Staring into the dark, the raiders looked into their own dark thoughts. That shot must have warned the Groslands, and they were three tough, no-run kind of men.

They had planned to start with the York place and then work on east, but now Burnine said they would by-pass York for the time being.

Dismounted, they crept in on Ernst's shack. They took too much time scouting to suit Burnine. He crashed through the door with his pistol in hand and dived to the floor.

There were still a few glowing embers in the fireplace. "They've caught on, sure enough," Burnine said. "Neither of them Grosland boys is the kind to run home to pa for no good reason."

They left Jordan to fire the place and rode on to William's cabin at the base of a hill. He had cut all but a few trees on the west side of it, so that it stood on open ground, except for brush, especially dense on the hill above the structure. The raiders closed slowly, crawling the last fifty feet or so until there was no more good cover between them and the cabin, about a hundred feet away.

Satisfied that his men were in place, with the ends of the skirmish line curling to cover the sides of the cabin, Burnine called out, "Grosland! Bring your boys out of there and we won't shoot!" There was no answer. Burnine called again. Pressed to the ground, the raiders listened to the silence. They were under strict orders not to fire until Burnine gave the word, and then to shoot low through the flimsy door, raking the floor of the cabin.

For five minutes the raiders strained to hear some noise from the cabin. It might be empty. Some of them began to believe that it was. Jake McAllister was on the right end of the line. Using stumps as cover, he wriggled over to the back corner of the cabin and put his ear close to the unchinked logs. He heard a hoarse whisper inside.

Jake retreated carefully and went down the line to tell Burnine that someone was inside. Burnine called out for the Groslands to surrender, and when only silence came back, he yelled, "Fire!"

Twelve men raked the bottom of the door with rifle, pistol and shotgun fire. There was no return. They kept firing, lighting the bushes with orange flashes and rocking the night with gunsmoke thunder until the bottom half of the narrow door was falling apart. Watching the gushing muzzle flames from the curving line of attackers, Burnine began to sense something fishy in the lack of return fire.

"Don't expose yourselves, men!" he shouted.

Clem Pettigrew heard the order but he had grown tired of lying flat while reloading his single shot carbine. He knelt on one knee and fired across a stump, probing blindly to get his lead through gaps between the logs near the corners of the cabin.

Ernst Grosland marked Pettigrew's gun flashes well because they were higher above the ground than any of the rest. He could hear the lead chunking into the heavy logs, and every time he raised himself to take a quick look through his loophole he expected to get a slug right in the eye.

The interior of the cabin was double-walled

with logs three feet above the floor and all the way around the interior, with more logs piled to the same height against the door. At intervals in all four walls were loopholes. Except for those now in use, the openings were plugged with tight-fitting pieces of wood.

The Groslands' plan of defense did not end with the stout cabin. After William had gone hell-for-leather to his father's house, a twelve-year-old sister had ridden at once to Harve Stenhouse's place, and now Big Harve and his son Joe Bob were lying in the brush on the hill above the cabin. The firing and the excitement had caused Joe Bob to wet his pants.

"Just lay low and wait," Big Harve told his son. "When we hear shotguns, we'll know the Groslands are in business. Time enough for us to get into then."

"Ye-yes—sir," Joe Bob said. "Maybe they're all dead in the cabin."

"Not by a damn sight."

The firing against the cabin began to drop off. Frank Jordan joined the raiders then, coming in on the right flank, giving the password in a hoarse whisper. He worked his way along the line to where Burnine was lying.

"Did you get that place burned?" Burnine asked.

"It's burning." Jordan was beginning to think less and less of the whole affair. Destroying homes while you were fighting a war was one thing. He had not liked it then. It was a downright miserable thing now.

"Damn it," Jake McAllister said. "We either got them or they ain't in there."

"You're the one who heard them talking inside," Burnine snapped. "Why don't you go have another listen?"

"I guess they're inside, all right, but if you ask me—"

"Nobody asked you," Burnine rasped. He stared along the dark ground at the dim bulk of the cabin. Like as not, the defenders had piled up something inside along the walls to help sponge up the bullets.

"Jordan, you work around and get on the hill," Burnine ordered. "Get some shots down through the roof at an angle to rake those front corners. Climb a tree if you have to."

Jordan felt his way up the hill. It was not high enough to give him the sharp angle of fire he needed. He was looking for a good tree to climb, wondering how he was going to climb it with his rifle, when he blundered into Big Harve Stenhouse.

Hearing the noise behind him, Big Harve pivoted on the seat of his pants, cocking his shotgun as he turned.

"Shiloh!" Jordan said hoarsely, thinking that someone else from the raiders' line had come up the hill, but even as he called out, he dropped flat.

"Shiloh your ass!" Big Harve roared, and fired one barrel.

Buckshot clipped the bushes above Jordan. He scrabbled away as fast as he could. He was behind a rock when Big Harve let the second barrel go, from a standing position. Soft lead spattered the stone. Jordan kept going. He didn't know how many hornets were in the nest he had disturbed.

Big Harve's first shot broke things open. Lying in the right front corner of the cabin, Ernst Grosland had had enough of the carbine flaming above the stump. When he heard Big Harve's shot on the hill, he jerked both triggers of his shotgun.

Clem Pettigrew had risen to reload, careless because there had been no fire from the cabin. Ernst's buckshot caught him high in the chest and throat. He fell forward over the stump, clawing the ground as blood choked him.

Surprised by the sudden fire from two places, the raiders were silent for a while. During those few moments they heard a ghastly whistling, bubbling sound from Pettigrew's shattered throat. Pettigrew was dead when Toby McAllister crawled over to him a few minutes later.

Wild with anger, Toby emptied his pistol at the cabin. Ernst fired back, one barrel this time. Most of the buckshot went into Pettigrew's body, still draped across the stump.

"Hold it!" Fred Grosland told his sons. "Wait for a rush."

The raiders were not about to rush the cabin. They had been shaken by the knowledge that they had enemies on the hill. Burnine, however, recovered quickly. He had recognized Big Harve's voice. Jordan must have stumbled into him, and now no doubt Jordan was dead.

"On the hill, you men!" Burnine yelled. "Close in behind Stenhouse and those others!" Someone on his left fired three rifle shots blindly up the hill and that gave Burnine a chance to enlarge his bluff. "Stop that, you idiot! You'll hit one of our own men up there!"

Big Harve was not the panicky kind. He thought that Burnine might be bluffing, but still . . . One man, at least, had tried to creep up behind him. There damn well could be more. Surprise was lost. There was nothing to be gained by staying any longer. Big Harve got his son and they retreated back to their horses.

Jordan heard the Stenhouses retiring, and speeded their going with a few shots, which added to the confusion of the raiders below. They didn't know what was happening on the hill, they felt that they were exposed, and they knew that the cabin was too tough. Burnine tried to hold them in place, but they fell back into the trees until they could stand up in safety.

The consensus was that they had seen enough of the Groslands for one night.

"We can root them out if we stay here till

morning," Burnine said. "Come daylight, we can get them."

"How about Big Harve and his bunch up there on the hill?" Matt Pilcher asked.

Before Burnine could answer, Jordan returned to report that, as far as he could tell, there had been only one man with Big Harve, and that both of them had high-tailed.

"That does it!" Matt cried. "Now they'll rouse the whole country. If we hang around here all night, they'll hit Shad's place, or yours, Burnine."

Burnine gave way grudgingly. "Before we quit, though, let's get York's cabin. Jake, you take six men and do that job. The rest of us will stay here and hold the Groslands down."

Jake picked his men and left. Burnine went forward to parley with the Groslands about recovering Pettigrew's body. He stayed behind a tree and kept calling out his request until Fred Grosland answered, "Stay where you are until I think it over. If there's any shooting in the meantime, you can go to hell."

It seemed incredible that the Yorks would be asleep, but from within came the sounds of two people snoring loudly. There was no lock on the door. Someone eased it open, lit a wadded bunch of dry grass and tossed it inside. The brief light showed Jeremy York and his huge wife snoring away in a pole bed.

Neither of them woke until the raiders were

crowding the room. Jake found the lamp and lit it. With his hair on end, York reared up in bed, blinking owlishly. "So you fellows did come, huh?"

Luke Pilcher checked the loft. "Nothing but kids up here."

His voice roused Mrs. York. She broke off a snore in the middle and stared at the visitors. "Why, they're uglier than I expected, Jeremy."

"This place burns in five minutes," Jake said.

Jeremy got up and dressed, and the children came tumbling down from the loft, curious and unfrightened, but Mrs. York refused to budge from her bed. Six men carried her outside, mattress, bedclothes and all, and put her into the wagon. Shad hitched the team. He was savage in his insistence that the Yorks could take anything they wanted. The raiders obeyed him. Their temper as a group had gone soft now, and they were more sullen than determined.

They piled the Yorks' possessions into the wagon, around the enormous woman lying there. She held the bedclothes up to her chin and kept giving orders about the things she wanted brought from the cabin.

The passive attitude of the family both puzzled and angered Shad. Someone said you were a cavalryman, York. That must have been a big lie."

"No. I was with Kilpatrick from here to there and then some. They made me a sergeant, and I was a good one, but after the war I seen the light.

I ain't no fighting man no more, but I'm stubborn when I'm in the right. You may as well hear it now, I'll be back."

"Then you'll be dead," Jake said.

"We all die sometime," York said calmly, "the meek and the violent. The Lord, not you, will decree my death."

Jake gave the little man a violent shove toward his wagon. "Climb up on that seat and git!"

York reeled against a hub and hurt his hip, but his dignity did not desert him, and neither would he be hurried. He took his time, lashing gear in the wagon so that it would not bump his wife, arranging a grass-filled mattress for his children to sit on. The raiders were already wrecking the cabin on top of a heap of dry wood. Someone lit the fire so they could see to do their work better.

Jordan paused beside a little girl who was holding a rag and stick doll. "Ain't you scared bad, sis?"

She had been watching the fire and the reflection of it was in her eyes as she looked at Jordan. "Evil can't hurt nobody, unless they got it in their own head, mister cowboy."

Jordan stared for a moment at the girl and then turned away quickly.

About the time the Yorks were ready to go, Burnine and his group rode into the firelight. Gifford was leading Pettigrew's horse with its dead owner lashed across the saddle.

"I'll drive careful like, Birdie," York told his wife.

"I'd appreciate that, Jeremy."

The wagon grated away into the darkness. "He's more dangerous than the Groslands," Burnine said.

With one dead man across his saddle, the raiders rode away from their shoddy victory. Not talking, suddenly moody, all they wanted was to separate from each other.

Their night was not yet finished.

When they reached the meadows of Little Creek, they saw fires they had not set.

"Oh Christ!" Toby cried. "That's my house!"

"And that blaze on the right is mine," Burnine said grimly.

They forgot about Shad, who was on foot. He did not care. He went on to the river and got his saddle and bridle from beside his dead horse. When he reached his yard, his wife challenged him from the dark shadows near the barn. "Who is it?"

"Katy! What are you doing out there?"

Shad's wife, his daughter, Bessie, and his daughter-in-law, Dorcas, came out of the gloom, carrying firearms.

"We figured we'd get a good crack at anybody who came skulking around to burn the place," Katy said.

"Does Toby know you came over here, Dorcas?" Shad asked.

"No. Katy came over to get me after—"

"Jesus Christ!" Shad ran to get a horse. When he was clear of the cottonwoods, he saw that it was not Burnine's house that was burning but his prized haystacks north of it.

The raiders, too, had seen as much, and so they had stayed at Toby's place. By the time Shad arrived, the others had done all they could. Sparks and embers from the burning house had fired the barn, but they had managed to get the tools and harness from it and to save a wagon that was threatened by the flames.

Toby had been like a wild man, thinking his wife and baby might still be in the house. He calmed down quickly after Shad told him that his family was safe.

There was a general cursing of the Stenhouses; it must have been they who came over and set the fires after Burnine bluffed them into retreating from the hill above Ernst Grosland's cabin.

Three men stayed at Toby's place to keep the fire from spreading into the trees. Matt Pilcher was one of them. His cracked ribs were hurting him so much that he said he could not do any fire fighting that required bending. Burnine took the rest of the raiders to see about his haystacks.

It had been a windless night but now a light breeze was running out of the west and it had thrown fire from the burning stacks across the fence and ignited dead grass and underbrush at the edge of the cottonwood grove near Burnine's house.

For the rest of the night the raiders fought to keep the fire from reaching Burnine's buildings. By then the Pilchers were wishing that they had never ridden south.

Frank Jordan leaned on his shovel and shook his head. "What a low-down bitch of a night." That seemed to reflect everyone's sentiments.

The Big Fire Raid was finished. By that name it became known in later years, when many different versions held that from ten to twenty buildings had been burned, and five to twelve men killed in desperate fighting.

Chapter Ten

Minor touches followed the main events of the Big Fire Raid.

After her father and others stopped briefly at the Burnine place to get tools to fight the haystack fires, Susan went out to see what the trouble was with a horse that was stamping restlessly and kicking at the corral.

Her eyes not yet adjusted to the darkness, she was feeling her way around the animal when she put her hand on Pettigrew's cold face. She screamed once and then ran terrified back into the house.

Jeremy York went three hundred yards before turning back to his burning cabin. He told Birdie he wanted to be on the ground for an early start rebuilding.

A half hour later Fred Stenhouse and Joe Bob came out of the night to see how the Yorks had fared, and found the whole family asleep, Jeremy lying under the wagon, rolled in an old army blanket.

In the light of the burning cabin Stenhouse looked at his son. "When he said he had faith in the Lord, he wasn't just talking idle, was he?"

After a few hours sleep and a hearty breakfast, Eben and Uriah Martin went fishing, figuring that they deserved some relaxation after their busy night.

They had looked Burnine's house over after the raiders left it to strike the Groslands. It appeared that they had a good chance to make some big mischief, but the dead quiet of the place made them uneasy. Old Burnine was tougher than a Comanche shield and full of trickery. It was hardly likely that he would leave his house unprotected. Ever since they had killed his dogs, the Martins had been leery of getting too close to his place for fear of some hellish trap, and the longer they stood in the dark and thought about it, the more real it seemed.

Gunfire southeast of Little Creek gave them a good excuse to leave. When they were close to

Toby McAllister's place, they could hear the shooting very plainly. Uriah laughed. "If we wanted that kind of war, Eben, we could've joined the army. Listen to that, will you!"

They were still lurking in the trees when Katy McAllister came to get her daughter-in-law and grandchild. After that, their course of action was clear. They set Toby's cabin on fire. Dorcas had made somewhat of a pet of the calf in the corral with its mother. It followed along the rails as Uriah went toward the barn.

Uriah was struck with sudden inspiration. He reached through the poles, scratching the calf under the jaw, and then he cut its throat with his hunting knife and dragged the still-kicking animal out under the bottom poles. "Give me a hand, Eben. We'll leave a burnt sacrifice for that Toby bastard."

Together the brothers heaved the calf on the flames.

"Listen to that old cow bawl," Eben said. "Let's get out of here and see what we can do with Jake's place."

"Let's not be greedy, brother Eben. For one night, we've done good. Maybe we've got time to catch them haystacks of old Burnine's on our way home."

"I'll bet you we do have the time," Eben laughed.

With the haystacks burning nicely, the Martins

retired to a hill, and from there they viewed with pleasure fires all over the land. The burning of Ernst's cabin and then the York home gave them about as much satisfaction as their own handiwork.

It was all destruction.

When the grove caught fire from the haystacks, they laughed and whacked each other on the back. They were getting a bonus they hadn't figured on.

After a time they prudently went to their homes, where they rubbed their horses dry with handfuls of crisp grass. They left their saddle blankets outside, so they could say, if anyone came to inquire, that the dampness of the blankets came from the morning dew.

They need not have worried in the least about having demanding callers, for the Stenhouses were getting the blame for what the Martins had done.

No one at the Shad McAllister ranch was sleeping, except Dorcas' baby. Bessie offered to share her room with Dorcas, but the latter knew she couldn't sleep for thinking of her burned home, so she helped her mother-in-law cook an early breakfast, while Toby and Shad engaged in a wild argument with Jake, who wanted to go at daylight to kill Big Harve and Joe Bob Stenhouse.

"We don't know that it was them who burned Toby's place!" Shad kept yelling.

Alone in her room, Bessie listened to the bitter

wrangling with a feeling of despair. There was little chance that she and Joe Bob could get married. Not now.

The Ute Calf Runner, camped in Burnine's grove, became uneasy when so many white men rode back and forth near his lodge. He heard the shooting at William Grosland's place. He scouted downriver and saw the Martins burning Toby's cabin. Calf Runner was not interested in the wars of the white men, but he knew that their craziness and hatred often spilled over on Indians.

At daylight he took his family and moved to Deer Valley, setting up his lodge below O'Neal's cabin, in the cottonwoods beside the creek. Major was a good white man who would welcome Calf Runner, and leave him alone. Burnine was a good white man too, but now he was warring with his brothers and so it was best to stand away from him.

O'Neal, who had visited Calf Runner's camp in company with his son, the Angry One, was the best of all the white men. His thinking was good. He spoke the old language. Already this summer he had visited Ute lodges in many places, camps that the other white men did not even know about. O'Neal was of the mountains. He was at peace with them, like the Utes, and he had returned to them to leave his bones.

It had pleased Calf Runner to reach his new camp by following old trails along the Arkansas, secret routes among the broken hills and rocks, where white men did not know the way. Coming up from the river, he set his lodge where he wanted it, and Major didn't even know he was there.

Chapter Eleven

In spite of the aches and complaints of his body, Major forged ahead stubbornly with the building of his storehouse. He was setting the teeth of his handsaw when the Pilchers rode by shortly before noon.

They were a begrimed and tired looking bunch. Matt was sitting very straight in his saddle. He gave Major a sour go-to-hell look and said nothing, and none of the rest of them spoke.

Silent and sullen, Major thought. By God, that suited him just fine.

It began to rain shortly afterward. Smoke from the fireplace chimney curled down over the roof and ran in a cloud across the yard. The rain settled in as a steady drizzle.

Major was cooking dinner when Frank Jordan rode into the yard, driving the bull that Burnine had promised to sell Major some time before.

Major went out and helped herd the bull into the oxen shed.

Frank Jordan stayed for dinner. Major scarcely

knew him, though he had seen him around Burnine's a few times, a slightly built young dark-haired man with a friendly grin and not much else to distinguish him.

Jordan told him about the trouble the night before. "It's funny how you get excited when you start out on something like that, but before it wound up, the whole thing had run pretty thin with me. I'm sort of glad old Burnine tied a can to my tail, because this thing is just started."

"Did you scare out?" Major asked. "Is that why he canned you?"

Jordan gave him a steady look. "No. There was a lot of it that didn't suit me, but I didn't scare out."

"What did happen?" Major asked carefully.

Jordan shook his head.

"I've got a reason for asking," Major said.

Jordan studied him for a moment. "As near as I can figure, it must have been because I shot off my mouth about having such a great time with General Sherman down in Georgia. I know that don't quite make sense, but—"

"Oh, man!" Major said. "That makes great sense. Burnine had kin down there. His cousin put up a sign saying that no hogs or Yanks could be buried on his land. Sherman's men hung him and his wife went crazy and drowned herself in a well."

"Oh, hell," Jordan murmured. "I didn't know." He looked at Major warily. "That's right, you're pretty close to him. Well, it wasn't all good in that war. Some of our bummers got hung too."

Jordan rose from the table, glancing at the rain. "I thank you for the meal, and now I'll be getting along."

"Wait a minute," Major said. "Something troubles me. Burnine fired you but still you drove the bull up here for him."

"Burnine paid me for the full month." Jordan shrugged. "Delivering the bull was no great chore."

"Where you headed?"

"I don't know." Jordan sat down slowly.

Major made him the same proposition he had offered Chunk and Burt Pilcher and O'Neal. Jordan listened carefully and then he said, "You think that'll work? You think you're going to avoid trouble?"

"No," Major said. "I expect some trouble."

Jordan studied him keenly for a time. Then he rose and walked out of the cabin and Major thought he had lost him. A few moments later Jordan returned with his warbag and blanket roll. "I ain't saying I'll stay any five years, Whitlock, but I'll give it a try until next summer. All right?"

"Fair enough."

The rain was coming steadily. Out in the shed the bull was bellowing like a lonesome buffalo. "Take that bull up to where my cows are, Jordan," Major said. "You'll find them about two miles west in the aspen parks."

Jordan hesitated a moment. Major met his look steadily and tried to hide the uncertainty he felt in giving the order. Then Jordan said, "All right." He rose and put on his poncho.

Major looked through the north window, past the rain drip from the eave, at the tall-grass meadows. Just what was the magic appeal in the ownership of land? He had told himself and others too that he loved the valley, but now he wondered if it was that, or was it that he *wanted* the valley and everything else around it that he could clutch and keep, so he could say with selfish pride, "This is mine. I own it."

How much was it going to cost before he really owned it?

Wet to the hide in spite of his army poncho, Jordan came in two hours later, water dripping from his hat, his boots squishing as he walked across the dirt floor to the fireplace. "I found your cows. The bull is with them."

"How many?"

"Five, with calves."

"See any steers?"

"I didn't look," Jordan said. "Was I supposed to?"

"No. I just wondered. I've had a couple of them shot lately."

Jordan held his hands to the fire and said nothing.

"I'd like to know what you think is going to

happen in this country, after last night," Major asked.

Jordan shook his head. "If Burnine and Toby McAllister and that bunch—Toby's your brother-in-law, ain't he?"

"That's right."

"If they killed the Stenhouses, this morning, like they went to do, I'd say anything could happen from now on."

"They went—Oh, Jesus! Why didn't you tell me that?"

With the front of his poncho steaming, Jordan turned his back to the fireplace. "They left just before I started up here with the bull."

"Do you figure Joe Bob and his pa burned Toby out and set those haystacks on fire?" Major asked.

"Jake McAllister and Burnine figure it that way. That's what counts."

Major paced the floor. "They burn all those places you said, and they try to kill the Groslands, but when one of *their* houses gets hit, they go shoot someone in cold blood. This whole thing is wrong, I tell you!"

"Yeah." Jordan took off his poncho and hung it on a peg. "From what I seen of Big Harve, they may have hard luck killing him."

Major kept telling himself that he was completely apart from the miserable conflict, and that he was going to stay that way.

By lamplight at the long table that night Major

sketched the salient features of the land above the claim that Burt and Chunk were holding. Jordan watched him work and thought, "The man has a good eye for topography. That's a better map than some we tried to follow during the war."

Major decided to let the north mesa remain open ground. One thing at a time.

"Four forties right across here, Jordan. That'll put a stopper at the head of this valley and take in a big chunk of the land you rode across today. First thing in the morning, we'll pick a place for you to build your cabin."

"How much of the time do I have to stay there?"

"You're supposed to live on the land for anyway five months out of the year. We'll make it stick if you're there even a part of that time. Possession is what counts."

Frank Jordan wondered if the same sort of thing was happening to him that had happened once before, when he rushed away to enlist in the cavalry, or, at the very least, the artillery. That he wound up in the infantry was entirely due to the influence of an ambitious man who needed to raise an infantry regiment in order to get a colonel's commission.

Jordan found that out later during his fast transition from a green Pennsylvania farm boy to a battle-scarred corporal.

This time, however, he had a fair idea of what he was getting into. He'd learned that men came in every grade, no matter what they wore on their shoulders. When you found a good one, that was the fellow to tie to.

This Major Whitlock was a good one. Young as he was, he had the mark of knowing what he was doing, and that, Jordan knew from four years of war, was a rare and remarkable quality. Ever since the war, Jordan hadn't known what he was doing and didn't much care, though occasionally he had given brief consideration to his shiftlessness.

Without any disturbing ambition of his own Jordan still could recognize ambition in another man. Whitlock had it, you could bet. If he didn't let it lead him into thinking he could whip a whole regiment with a scout detail, he just might go a long way.

Jordan was willing to string along with him. There was satisfaction in being well led.

Though it was still drizzling rain the next morning, they went above the head of Deer Valley and picked a site for Jordan's claim cabin, against a wall of tall aspens on the south fork of the creek. "If you can find enough sound dead stuff in that thicket, you won't have to fight green logs," Major said.

"Yeah, I know." Jordan took off his jacket and picked up the axe.

Major went back to finish his storeroom. Riding down the south mesa, he observed how the rain had freshened up the sparse bunch grass. The whole mesa now looked green in the misty rain.

The next chore he had to get done was digging ditches. He could move Chunk Pilcher up here and have him build a cabin. No need for both Chunk and Burt to hold down one claim in the valley. Then, in time, he would find someone else for the north mesa.

With his mind churning with plans for the future, Major rode down the hill and found Jim Goodwin waiting for him at the cabin. If there was anyone that Major was always glad to see, it was the big storekeeper. "I was just about to go looking for you," Goodwin said. "Meanwhile I made some coffee. Good Lord, Major, do you ever change grounds?"

Major grinned. "Can't afford to. I keep boiling the same pot of grounds until they turn to silt."

"So did I, before I married your mother. That reminds me, I brought you a new coffee mill, best little thing you ever saw."

Major dutifully examined and praised the coffee mill. It was a pretty thing, with an ivory knob on the handle, and with painted elephants marching around the sides of the box. Polly would really be tickled with something like that, Major thought.

Being inside always made Goodwin restless. He stomped over to the doorway and looked outside. "I guess you understand the trouble we're facing. That's what I came here to talk about."

"I can't stop it, Mr. Goodwin. I'm going to watch out for myself."

Goodwin swung around quickly. "The Groslands were taking care of themselves when they killed Clem Pettigrew. The bunch that tried to kill the Groslands were also taking care of themselves. So was Burnine and the whole outfit that went over to kill the Stenhouses, yesterday morning, and the Stenhouses were taking care of themselves by not being there.

"How many more men do you want killed over this business of looking out for themselves? All of us have to think a little beyond that sort of thing, or this country will wind up dark and bloody ground. Is that what we want, Major?"

"I didn't start the trouble."

"Nobody did, but we've got it just the same, and no one, including you, can take a stand-off position and expect to come out clean and unhurt," Goodwin said earnestly.

"I'll get hurt a damn sight worse if I get into it!"

Goodwin took a deep breath. "I'm not talking about taking sides. I'm talking about getting together and trying to work out our differences."

"The Pilchers? All the others? Fat chance!"

"There's a very good chance."

"It's too late now."

"It's not too late, believe me!" Goodwin put both hands flat on the table and leaned toward Major. "The trouble night before last has sobered up some of those who were in it. They see now what this dog-eat-dog business will lead to."

"*Some* of them, huh?"

"That's where anything starts, with *some*. All day yesterday and most of last night, I've been going around talking to people. I saw the McAllisters, the Groslands, Burnine, the Stenhouses." Goodwin didn't mention that Joe Bob, edgy and scared, had taken a shot at him and killed his horse as Goodwin was approaching the cave where Joe Bob and Big Harve were hiding. "The Martins were out in the hills somewhere, their wives said. They'd been gone for three or four days. I'll see them tomorrow if they're back.

"On the way up here, I saw Sherman and Lavington. I'll talk to the Pilchers today and the Sheplers."

"Then there's Gifford, but I sure wouldn't depend on him for anything," Major growled.

"Personal likes and dislikes don't enter into this. We've got to have a broader view than that."

Major toyed with his tin cup. He had a feeling that Goodwin was trying to ease him into something. "How did all these people take your talk?"

"Why, they argued and raised hell, of course, at the very idea of getting together. I could have had a fight everywhere I went. Even Tad Sherman was that mad at first. After they ran out of steam, they let me get in a few words, and pretty soon most of them agreed that we'd better have a truce meeting. That's all I asked, just that they come to the store for a talk."

"Burnine agree?"

Goodwin nodded.

"The McAllisters?"

"Toby and old Shad. Jake was one of the few that never did cool down, but he'll be there."

"Lavington?"

"He's willing to talk. He was all for it."

It had been a mistake to ask questions, Major decided, for it had shown that he had an interest in the matter that he didn't want to admit.

"Right at this moment you're probably the most respected man in the country, Major."

"Me?"

"Possibly the most disliked too, by the folks who figure you should be on their side. You see, you've stood back and let everyone else run his neck into a noose, and right now they hate you for it but at the same time they feel respect for you too."

Major couldn't quite believe it.

"We need you badly at the meeting I'm getting together at the store next Saturday," Goodwin said.

Major didn't like it in the least. He had done very well by himself so far. But there was Lafait to consider. If trouble ever struck Deer Valley, Lafait would be marked for the kill first off . . .

"backed up by that murdering brother of

yours." . . . In anger, Toby McAllister had had the guts to say that to Major's face.

How many others were saying it behind his back?

Still, Major hesitated. "Suppose I do go to your meeting and say just what I think, that everybody has to look out for himself?"

"Do you really believe that?" Goodwin asked gently.

"As far as it concerns me, yes!"

"That's the thing to say then, if you think it will help keep this country from having a senseless, bloody war."

"You're trying to mix me up, Mr. Goodwin."

"No, I'm just trying to lean on you for some help. Will you please come to the meeting?"

Major scowled. "What day is today?"

"It's Saturday. The meeting will be just a week from now."

"Why so far away?"

"There will be a lot of cooling off between now and then."

"Or more shooting and burning," Major grumbled.

"I don't think so. One man is dead, the Regulators have made a stand-off, at least, and some of the people on the other side are beginning to get a little common sense."

Goodwin was a fine man, and when it came to being his brother's keeper, he went farther than just words, but maybe he was trying to do something so big it was impossible. Get all those stubborn, angry people together and make them agree on anything? "Do you think your idea will work, Mr. Goodwin?"

"Yes! One meeting won't work a miracle but it will be a start. The idea that men can settle their differences peacefully *will* work. Are you going to be there, Major?"

"You know what people will say, don't you? They'll say you're trying to act like God so the country won't have a bad name, so people won't be afraid to come here to settle, so you can sell more things from your store and lots in your town-site and lumber from your mill—"

"That's all been said already, to my face." Goodwin smiled. "Do you believe it? I mean, do you think that's the only reason I'm trying to do something?"

"No."

"Thank you. Then you'll come to the meeting?"

"All right, all right!" Jeem's cousin! Goodwin never gave up.

Goodwin walked to the door. For the first time Major observed that he was limping slightly. "What's the matter with your leg, Mr. Goodwin?"

"Just a bruise, that's all. A horse went down with me. By the way, we've got a doctor in the country now. His name is Kimball." Goodwin went out and got on his horse.

"Hey! That's Joe Bob's horse," Major said.

"Yes." Goodwin smiled. "He was good enough to lend it to me after he shot mine." He rode away and left Major staring after him with a puzzled expression.

Lafait returned late at night the day that Major finished his storehouse and moved most of the plunder from the south wall of the cabin.

Except for being red-eyed, dusty and beard-stubbled, Lafait didn't look much like a mule-skinner when he stumbled into the cabin. He was wearing a new hat and a new dark broadcloth suit, and his white shirt was mighty fancy, and mighty dirty too.

"Stayed a little longer than I planned," he said. "So I drove damn near day and night when I could. Do you suppose you could put that mule team away for me?"

Major dressed and went out in the moonlight. It was a big wagon and about the largest pair of mules Major had ever seen. They were too tall to put in the oxen shed, so he picketed them out on the meadow.

Lafait was asleep when Major went inside. One brand-new boot was on the table and one was lying on the floor. Scattered across the table, as if Lafait had thrown it from a distance, was money in bills and gold pieces.

Major gathered it up and counted it. More than

six hundred dollars. He stuffed it into Lafait's boot. . . . *driving day and night*. . . . On the run? My God, had Lafait got into some kind of trouble?

Major tried to rouse him, and got nowhere. It was not easy to shake Lafait out of sleep the next morning at daylight, but at last he swung out of the bunk, put on his hat and yawned his way over to the table to drink coffee.

"That's some fancy underwear," Major said.

"Ain't it just? I never knew a man could get so dirty driving a wagon."

"Where'd the money come from, Lafait?"

Lafait cocked one eye and grinned. "Old mother hen Maje. There you go, thinking right off that I must have held up a stagecoach."

"Where'd you get it?"

Lafait gulped his coffee. "I didn't hold up no stagecoach. I robbed a Wells-Fargo office."

"You—you—what!"

Lafait began to laugh. "This land-grabbing business is making an old grandpa out of you, Major. I won the damn money in a poker game at Jenny Auden's place."

"What kind of place is that?"

"They hold revival meetings there."

"Oh, I see." Major grinned.

"She's some woman. I told her about you. She said she'd like to meet you sometime. When you go to Denver, drop in at the New Orleans and tell her who you are."

"I'll start today. What are you going to do with the money, Lafait?"

"How much is there?"

"Six hundred and thirty-nine dollars."

"I had more than that once, and then I hit a bad streak. Hell, I ain't going to do anything with it, Maje. I brought it back for you to keep this place going."

Major stared at his brother. "It's a loan, understand?"

"All right, all right! Whatever you say." Lafait poured another cup of coffee. He walked to the door with it in his hand. "If you don't mind cooking me some breakfast, I'll just waddle down to the crick and have myself a bath." He went out, drinking the coffee as he walked slowly toward Deer Creek.

During breakfast, Major told him what had happened while Lafait was gone. Since he would hear it somewhere soon enough, Major gave him the straight of his fight with Toby McAllister and with the Pilchers.

A quietness settled in Lafait's expression and the dark glints showed in his eyes. "What do you want to do about the Pilchers?"

"Nothing."

"Gifford?"

"He wasn't even in it. I hit him with a board because he was handy. I wouldn't mind hitting him again."

"I met the Pilchers that day," Lafait said slowly. "I told them I was headed for Denver, so they just rode on down here and decided—"

"It's all over. I won't forget it, but it's over."

"You're a damn fool to fight with your fists, Maje."

"I know. You've told me that before." Major changed the subject. "What do you think about the burnings?"

Lafait shook his head. "I don't think Goodwin will ever get the two sides to agree."

"It could happen," Major said hopefully. "Goodwin is awful good at persuading folks to see things clear."

"Yeah. He'll be awful good at chewing on me, and Ma will be awful good at asking me questions I don't want to answer, if I don't get down there with that wagon pretty quick."

Lafait was wearing his new hat when he drove away. The rest of his fancy outfit was thrown on his bunk, and except for the headpiece he was dressed in working clothes.

Major watched the powerful mules take the heavy wagon with ease up the steep road to the south mesa. There was about two and a half tons of merchandise in the wagon, Lafait had said.

That Goodwin was something. The country was in a turmoil. Everyone was buying on credit, including Goodwin himself, and if the trouble didn't get leveled out someway, a heap of folks who owed Goodwin would be driven away.

But Goodwin, he was going full steam ahead, even to believing he could get a bunch of savages like the Pilchers to love their enemies.

Major felt the healed cut on his cheek. There were a few puckery places where Polly's stitches had been, but he guessed that if that was the worst he got out of the trouble the country was in, he'd be downright lucky.

It was high time to start on the bedroom and the kitchen. Thanks to Lafait, he could pay his lumber bill, and a few others, including something on what he owed Burnine.

Chapter Twelve

Katy McAllister chunked wood into the fire under the big copper tub in her yard. She was a tall, gaunt woman, with her coppery hair bunched in a big knot at the back of her neck. "Well, Major, you must have got up before breakfast to get here so early."

"I'm going to that truce meeting this afternoon so I thought I'd come down a little early and see if there was anything I could do to help Dorcas and Toby."

"Hmmn." Mrs. McAllister lit her short-stemmed pipe, plucking a coal from the fire under the wash water and juggling it in her palms before plopping it into the bowl of her pipe. "They're all over there at Toby's place, the mistopher and Bessie too. Like as not, they got it rebuilt by now. You know the McAllisters." Without pausing she asked, "What did you do to your cheek?"

Major felt his cheek. It hadn't been itching until Mrs. McAllister mentioned it. He was of a mind to lie about the cut, thinking that maybe Toby hadn't told his folks about the fight, but he was a poor liar and he knew it, so he said, "Me and Toby had a little scuffle. I supposed you knew."

"The big-mouthed Pilchers did mention it, I guess, but what with all the hell going on day and night, I can't keep track of things. What are you going to do at this here truce meeting of Goodwin's?"

"I don't know."

Mrs. McAllister felt the wash water. She pushed more wood under the tub. "Shad wants peace. He ought to. He fought Indians before the war, got shot in the butt during the war, and he's been fighting ever since to make us a ranch out here. He wants peace. Toby does too, I think. Jake, he's different. How do you feel?"

"Well," Major said cautiously, "nobody's going to win, the way things are going. I sort of favor Goodwin's idea, though I don't know much about it yet."

"So do I. So does your ma and Mrs. Burnine and everybody else with any sense. You may not know it, but Bessie and Joe Bob Stenhouse was a-figuring to get married. Now I've got a girl on my hands with the vapors, and the mistopher and the boys are fighting like dogs all the time.

"That Jeremy York went right back when they burned him out. Jake wants to go kill him. The mistopher says no. Jake wants to kill the Stenhouses for burning Toby's place. Then Bessie squalls like a calf. I ain't had a minute's peace this livelong summer, I tell you. You and Jim Goodwin are the only men in the country who've showed any common sense so far. When you go to that meeting, Major, you straighten things out, hear me?"

"Well, I—"

"You raise your voice loud and clear. They'll listen to you, I know. Where's Lafait?"

"Goodwin sent him to Denver. Something about a part for the sawmill." Like as not, Ma had her hand in that deal.

"How's Jude?"

"All right, last I heard."

"You speak up, understand? You rare up on your hind legs, Major Whitlock, and make those wild-eyed bastards hear some reason. Now I'll tell you. . . ."

Mrs. McAllister gave Major a heap of advice. When she ran down, he said he had to get over to see Dorcas.

Major's nose crinkled at the odor of the pile of

charred debris the McAllisters had cleared from the cabin site. With their usual hell-bent drive they had done a power of work already.

The cabin walls were up and Shad and Toby were putting the roof on, while Dorcas and Bessie McAllister were handing them up boards. Jake was trimming logs for a new barn.

He was the only one who did not pause in his work to greet Major.

"There's nothing so bad as the smell of a burned house," Dorcas said. "Especially your own." She was slender, almost delicate looking, with golden hair.

It occurred to Major that she was no longer a pretty girl but a downright beautiful woman. Just to glance at her, you might not realize it, but she had a heap of enduring, wiry strength in her slender body. Beside her, Bessie McAllister looked fat and tired.

Major went over to look at his nephew, King. The baby was asleep on blankets under a tree. A real fair chunk of youngun, Major allowed. "By gosh, he's getting to look like Toby."

Toby was pleased. "He'd damn well better," he said, grinning.

Major laughed, but he knew he'd made a mistake. From the corner of his eye he caught the quick, bitey look Dorcas flashed at him. He hadn't meant no more than what he'd said, but it was awful easy to offend Dorcas by making any kind of remark that she could take to remind her that she'd been with Bill Gifford before she married Toby.

"Sure a fine boy," Major said, and turned back to Toby. "I came by to see if there was anything I could do to help."

With his eyes on Major's scarred cheek, Toby looked sort of ashamed. He didn't need to be, Major thought. Toby had stood astraddle of him and scared the Pilchers off like an old boar coon defying a pack of half grown dogs.

"I sure do thank you," Toby said, "but there just ain't nothing you can do to help right now. You see—"

"I suppose you came down mainly to go to the meeting at Goodwin's," Jake said, still chopping away.

"I figure on it, yes."

There was an awkward moment of silence. Shad blew his nose vigorously, wiped the side of his hand across his nose, and then brushed the hand on his pants. "Me and the boys are going."

"Yeah, we're going." Jake stopped working. "We've got business there. What I don't understand is why you're going, Major."

"Don't start that again, goddamn it," Shad said wearily. "Major is about the only man in the whole country, besides Goodwin, that's shown any common sense."

"Are you and old Goodwin going to propose

we bring in a man from the land office to settle things?" Jake asked. "Is that what you got up your sleeve, Major?"

"That's about the last thing any of us could stand, I'd say." Major was doing his best to hold his temper. It wasn't easy with Jake on the prod.

"Oh, you'd come out smelling like a rose," Jake said. "What with the ten or fifteen people you've hired to hog the whole country up your way, and with old killer Lafait to back you up—"

"Goddamn you, Jake," Major said, and started toward him.

"Whoa!" Shad grabbed Major and it was like having a bear put the wrap-around on him. "Jake, you keep your mouth shut or I'll show you that you ain't near big enough yet to keep from being licked!" Shad roared.

Jake drove the double-bitted axe into a log. "Let him loose, Pa, let him come ahead!"

All the McAllisters, including Bessie, were yelling, and Major was doing his best to get out of old Shad's powerful grip, when the brown-bearded man on a mule rode into the scene.

"If you don't mind my sticking my nose in, I'd say we've got enough new trouble in this land, without a family fight."

For a small man, the newcomer had about as deep and commanding voice as Major had ever heard. Major stopped struggling. Jake picked up his axe again, and Shad turned Major loose.

"This here's Doc Kimball," Shad said. "Major Whitlock, Doc."

Kimball dismounted and shook hands with Major. He was a wiry looking fellow, Doc Kimball, with sharp, squinty eyes and a big nose. Ma said any doctor west of the Mississippi always smelled of whiskey, but Major didn't detect any such odor on Kimball.

Kimball greeted the two women pleasantly and then walked over to have a look at the sleeping baby. "Remember, Dorcas, the first sign of summer complaint, and you send Toby on the gallop to get me."

"I remember what you said." Dorcas nodded. "He's been just fine, so far."

"What's the new trouble you mentioned, Doc?" Shad asked.

"First, the meeting at Goodwin's is called off." Kimball looked quietly at the waiting group. "Someone killed Tad Sherman last night. Shot him dead with a rifle when he stepped into a lighted doorway."

O Christ! Major felt sick. Big, easy-going Tad Sherman. A wife and three young girls.

"Who?" Jake shouted. "Who did it?"

"No one knows," Kimball said. "There was a disturbance among the horses in his corral. He stepped into the doorway to go out and someone shot him. That's all his wife could tell us."

There had been a steady rain for several hours

the previous night, Major thought. Even so, maybe O'Neal could read sign and make something of it. But Major had no idea where O'Neal was.

"Where were the two Lavington boys?" Toby asked.

Kimball shook his head slowly. "As Goodwin says, let's not go off half-cocked. He's sent Jed Caldwell up the river to get the sheriff. There will be an investigation and a coroner's inquest."

"Investigation, hell!" Jake shouted. "What do those politicians in the mining country care about us? Who came down to investigate after Pettigrew got killed?"

Kimball said dryly, "It's probably a good thing no one did come down on that deal."

"Where were Lavington's boys?" Toby repeated.

"Working for a mining outfit near Dayton," Kimball said. "They're still there, as far as we know."

"Yeah, as far as you know," Toby growled. "Where was Lavington?"

"He was home in bed. His wife and daughter verified that."

"Sure!" Jake said. "What else did you expect them to say? Me, I'm for going up there with a bunch—"

"Shut up!" Shad said. "If we left it to you, there wouldn't be a Regulator left alive in the whole country."

"There sure as hell wouldn't be any Yorks on our land," Jake said, "and Lavington wouldn't be getting away with what he did last night."

"Who said it was Lavington?" Shad growled. "Where's there any evidence?"

Shad and Jake fell into a bitter, loud quarrel. Major thought it a good time to leave, and so did Kimball. Only Bessie and Dorcas bothered to say good-bye.

"I'm going on to Burnine's and up to the Martins to tell them the meeting's called off," Kimball said as he and Major rode away. "You want to go with me? I'm not too sure where the Martins live, in spite of Goodwin's directions."

"You won't have any trouble finding their place." Major had a feeling that Kimball wanted to talk to him, but the news of Sherman's death had given Major an uneasy sensation. He felt an urgency to get back to Deer Valley without delay. "I'll ride a ways with you," Major said, "but I think I'd best get on home. Got work to do."

"Your mother went up to stay with Mrs. Sherman."

"Figured she would." Major paused. "Have you got any ideas you didn't mention back there?"

Kimball dug in the pocket of his corduroy coat. "Catch," he said, and tossed a misshapen piece of lead over to Major. "What do you make of that?"

Major studied the bullet carefully. About a

175

.36 caliber, he guessed. The old rifle gun that Lavington had given Miami Rusk was that size. "Pretty hard to say, the way it's beat up."

"It hit a rib, went through the heart, and lodged just under the skin of his back. I weighed it on Goodwin's gold scales. I'd say it was .36 caliber, deformed, but still all there. If we had the mold it came from, I could cast another bullet, compare the weights and damn near prove something."

"I suppose so." Major remembered one night when he had gone over to see Polly. Bask Lavington had made twenty bullets for the old rifle gun and was sitting at the table trimming the sprues with a knife.

Miami had that rifle now, however, and Lavington surely must have given him the mold too. Still, it was a worrisome thought.

A quarter mile from Burnine's place Major said, "I'll leave you now. If you follow the crick on your way to the Martins, the first main fork on the right will take you straight to their place."

Kimball started to say something, and then he nodded and rode on.

Two miles above Chico Brush Creek, Major met Bill Gifford riding south. Gifford stopped his horse and said, "I guess you heard the news?"

"About Sherman, yes."

"We'll have the coroner's inquest at his house this afternoon, if I get everyone rounded up in time." Gifford brushed his coat back sort of

176

carelessly to reveal a badge pinned to his shirt pocket.

"Sheriff!" Major couldn't help blurting it out.

Gifford grinned. "Sam Creighton resigned last week. I always got along pretty well with the mining people, so when the county commissioners met yesterday, they just up and appointed me to fill out the term."

Sonofabitch, Major thought. Outside of establishing two voting precincts in the lower end of the county, the commissioners had acted like nobody lived outside of the mining districts. Now they'd gone and appointed the biggest bastard in the whole country as sheriff.

"Is Jed Caldwell still up the river?" Major asked.

Gifford nodded. "He's probably on his way back now." He drew a paper from his pocket and made an important act of studying it. "He's on the coroner's jury."

"Who else?"

"Goodwin, old Ross Pilcher, Toby McAllister, Lonzo Rusk, and Burnine. That's a pretty good mixture, wouldn't you say?"

"Yeah." Major rode on.

To the surprise of no one, the verdict of the coroner's jury was that Tad Sherman had come to his death at the hands of a party or parties unknown. During her testimony Mrs. Sherman repeatedly stated that she did not, and never would believe that Brent Lavington had killed her husband.

They buried Sherman the next day. Most of the people from the southern part of the county were there, including Eben and Uriah Martin. Jeremy York spoke the words of the brief ceremony in a simple and moving manner, using only a few sentences to lecture his listeners to the effect that Sherman's death hopefully might temper the bitterness of the warring factions and lead them toward a peaceful solution to their problems.

The truce was there for the moment, with men from both sides intermingled shoulder to shoulder for the half hour of quietness.

Afterward, Major wanted to talk to Polly, but Burnine intercepted him as he was going toward her. She rode away with her parents and Burnine drew Major down to the corral. "I'm satisfied that Lavington didn't do it," Burnine said bluntly.

"I'm sure he wouldn't have done it."

Burnine rubbed the chipped flesh of his cheek. His eyes were hard and cold. "That isn't quite the point, though. He isn't directly responsible, but . . ."

He left the rest to Major to figure out. After a time Major said, "You mean you're still set on hanging him?"

"I didn't say that. I would advise you, though, to stay completely clear of him."

"I don't care to be told things like that, Mr. Burnine."

"Sure, you don't. Just think about it, that's all. How's that bull doing?"

"Fine. Now look, Mr. Burnine—"

"I said he was a good one. Excuse me, Major. I've got to see Mrs. Sherman before I leave."

Frank Jordan was waiting to ride home with Major. Jordan's cabin was completed now and he had been helping build the addition to Major's cabin.

"Go ahead," Major told him. "I'll be along directly."

He rode up to Lavington's. Bill Gifford's horse was tied at the corral. Lavington came to the doorway and invited Major to get down and come inside. Major dismounted but he stayed beside Smoke, fiddling with the reins. "I just wanted to see Polly for a minute."

She came outside a few moments later.

"I was wondering what I did the other day that made you mad at me," Major said.

"I'm not mad at you."

She was, though, Major knew; it was there in her attitude of withdrawn coolness.

"I thought I'd go up to the pool tomorrow morning."

"Oh?"

"Will you meet me there?"

Polly studied him quietly. It seemed to Major

179

that her attitude softened a little. "I don't know," she said. "I may have things to do but I'll think about it."

"Please." That was damn near begging, Major thought, and it sort of hurt his pride.

As he rode away he could hear Gifford talking. Gifford. The sheriff. Sonofabitch!

In the morning Major told Jordan that he was going to ride up toward Mt. Lebanon to check the cows. An hour later he climbed down to the lean-to near the warm pool.

The pine bough mattress in the shelter was starting to lose its needles. Cooking gear and other items he and Polly had left hanging on the trees had not been moved. A fine film of dust lay on the stepping stones they had laid to the pool.

Major stayed until the sun was reaching into the canyon from directly overhead.

Jordan was working on the stone foundation of the addition when Major returned. "How were the cows?"

"The cows? Oh, yeah—fine."

Major went to work with savage energy.

Chapter Thirteen

Jordan tapped his shovel against the top of a rock that was lying close to the outside of the cabin. "That either comes out, or we make this addition floor about eight inches higher than you figure, Major."

"Out she comes then."

The rock was like an iceberg, mainly under the surface, and two other rocks were keyed against it. By the time they got them out, there was a hole large enough to hold a man and it extended beyond the foundation line of the addition.

Jordan threw a few shovelfuls of dirt into it and then he stopped. "You know something? I'd just leave that pit. I'd make me a little trap door in the floor and cover the outside part of the hole with boards and dirt, and then I'd have me an ace in the hole when it came to getting out of the cabin without going through a door or window."

Two days before Major would not have thought much of the idea. An escape hole. Now he gave it serious consideration.

He had ridden over to Lavington's the previous night. Brent Lavington was not around when Major arrived, but he showed up a few minutes later, putting his rifle on pegs above the door. After that, Mrs. Lavington and Polly put blanket scraps over the two windows and lit the lamp.

Major saw heavy wooden shutters for the windows, leaning against the wall below the openings.

"What's been going on lately?" Major asked.

"Nothing," Lavington said. "That's what bothers me. How about some coffee, Polly?"

"When I get the fire going." She was uncovering coals in the fireplace.

They had raked ashes over the fire when dusk came, Major thought. He saw strain around Lavington's eyes. The man's awareness was cocked toward every small noise outside. And his wife looked tired and worried.

"Where's the boys?" Major asked.

"Still up at the mines," Lavington answered.

"I'm just as glad they're away," his wife said.

"I hear that those folks who got burned out are rebuilding, and nobody is bothering them," Major said. His eyes kept straying to Polly.

"Yes, yes." Lavington nodded bleakly. "Gifford came by yesterday. He said it was all love and sweetness down there on Little Creek."

The air of fear and tension infected Major. He thought of what Burnine had told him about staying clear of Lavington. There was a deep-running streak of cold determination in Burnine, and if he figured that killing Lavington would scare the daylights out of the rest of the Regulators, he would do just that.

But he would not come sneaking by night; or would he? He had led the Great Fire Raid by night.

Mrs. Lavington said, "We've talked of leaving, but Brent won't have it." She gazed at the lamp with a remote expression. "Mrs. Sherman and the girls are pulling out tomorrow, going back east to her folks."

Major never did get a chance to talk to Polly alone. When he started to leave, Lavington said, "Hold it!" and blew out the light before Major could open the door. For a while Major waited beside his horse, but Polly did not come out.

He looked at the dark trees on the hills, at the shadowy fields below the spring. There seemed to be an awesome, waiting quiet hanging all around Kettle Drum Springs.

Riding home on the old buffalo trail, he stopped several times, listening to the dark. I'll be damned if I'll huddle inside four walls like that, he thought.

But now, with Jordan waiting for an answer about the escape hole, Major said, "Let's do that." And he decided to make heavy shutters for the windows too.

They left the hole in the crawl space and covered the exit as Jordan had described. The following day they laid hewed log plates on the foundation and began to string joists, starting from the end where the escape hole was. By evening the floor was down. The trapdoor would be cut later.

The cabin was hotter than blazes when they quit work. Jordan started to build a fire and then he said, "What do you say we cook outside?"

They ate supper beside a small fire in the yard. Afterward, loath to go inside, they sat on a pile of lumber and watched night come to Deer Valley. Fawn and Steuben plodded up from the meadow to rub against the corner of the building, and then they went rumbling back to the grass.

A cool west wind came with the night. Major put more wood on the fire. "Sometimes I sure think O'Neal has the right idea, staying in the mountains all summer, not worrying about owning anything."

"For him, it's the right idea, maybe." Jordan cocked his ear suddenly, listening. "Speak of the devil. . . ."

O'Neal and Miami came out of the dusk, padding in almost silently on moccasined feet. "Have you eaten?" Major asked.

"Just et, thanks," O'Neal said.

"Set a spell."

O'Neal shook his head at Jordan's offer to get them boxes from the cabin. He and Miami sat on the ground. For a while Major thought O'Neal might have something on his mind, but the old man said nothing.

It came to Major that it was one of the rare and

mystic times when men were content to visit silently, sharing companionship without working at it. A fire in the open had some magic quality that brought it about; it never happened inside.

Sometime later, O'Neal startled everyone but Miami when he grunted a few words in Ute. A few moments later Calf Runner walked out of the darkness and sat down near Jordan.

"It's a good thing I never had to fight Indians," Jordan said. "I never even heard him."

"Where'd you come from, Calf Runner?" Major asked.

The Ute pointed down the valley.

"Been camped there for a long time." Miami glanced at Major as if to say he sure was dumb, and then he rose and put more wood on the fire.

For another ten minutes they sat silently. Then Calf Runner said something in Ute to O'Neal. They talked back and forth for a while. The others watched them curiously. When the conversation was finished, no one felt a need to inquire about it.

O'Neal said, "He came here to tell you that he saw the men who burned your sister's place, Major."

"Who?"

"I don't know the names. From what he says, I place the pair all right." O'Neal described the two men.

Eben and Uriah Martin.

The magic spell of the fire and the silent communion were broken.

"He's sure of what he saw?" Major asked.

"I wouldn't insult him by asking that," O'Neal growled. "He's your friend and he knows it was your sister's house and he knows what he saw. He ain't no white man trying to stir up trouble. He thought about it a long time before he decided to tell you."

Major wished Calf Runner hadn't made it such a public matter, but he couldn't blame him or O'Neal either, for neither of them cared a whit about the country's troubles.

Major nodded at the Indian. "Thanks."

Presently, the visitors walked away into the darkness.

After a while Major said irritably, "All I wanted to do was stay here in this valley and mind my own business, but it didn't work, and now, by God, even the Indians are dumping problems on me."

"That's the price of responsibility," Jordan said quietly.

"That's a big word," Major grumped, "and I ain't sure just how it's supposed to fit me." He struggled with the problem Calf Runner had handed him. If he told Toby, the McAllister tempers would run wild, and it wouldn't matter one bit that they themselves had been out that night burning cabins. Somebody would get killed.

"Suppose you don't say anything?" Jordan said.

That was the easiest course, sure enough, at first thought. Now there was peace and Major would like to keep it that way; but as he sat there beside the dying fire, strong in his mind was a hatred of bushwhackers that had been established during the war.

Scum. Cowardly, vicious scum who crept around the edges of honest fighting, preying on the helpless and the weak. "Did you ever hear the Martins talk about being in the war, on either side?"

"I never had more than a dozen words with them since I've been here. Why?"

"I'll bet you they was guerrillas."

"Maybe," Jordan said, "but you don't know that they was." He hesitated. "You're thinking that maybe they killed Sherman, ain't you?"

"Yes."

"That's a guess, Major," Jordan said. "Why would they?"

"I don't know. It looks like they would have picked Burnine or one of the McAllisters, instead of Tad Sherman. Sherman never had his heart in the trouble."

"Maybe that's what made him so careless, walking into a lighted doorway in the dead of night."

"You think the Martins did it, don't you, Jordan?"

"I didn't say that. I said that Sherman was easy pickings." Jordan looked over his shoulder suddenly, toward the dark grove of cottonwoods behind the cabin, and then Major found himself staring uneasily into the darkness.

He rose suddenly and got a bucket of water and extinguished the fire.

Why, it was getting to be like the war years when Ma wouldn't let there be a light after dusk for fear of attracting one of the wandering bands of bushwhackers.

Before he fell asleep Major wrestled with the problem of what to do with the information Calf Runner had given about the Martins. In the morning it was the first item on his mind after he awoke.

He had done his best to stay out of the trouble, and he still wanted it that way, but you just couldn't overlook what the Martins had done. They were not on either side, and that made them dangerous to everyone.

Until midmorning he worked with Jordan, and then, resenting the time it would cost him, but feeling obliged to do it, he decided to get O'Neal and have him question Calf Runner again. There might have been some misunderstanding.

O'Neal and Miami were not at their cabin. Major went on down the creek until he found Calf Runner's lodge. In a mixture of Spanish, English, and sign language, Calf Runner's wife explained that he and O'Neal and the Angry One had gone hunting.

Resenting even more the wasted time, Major rode back to his cabin. He decided that before he blundered into a mistake of some kind about the Martins, he had better ask Goodwin's advice. Goodwin would know what to do.

Coming up from the meadow, Major heard Polly talking to Jordan. He tried to keep from hurrying as he went around the cabin. She was sitting on her pony, laughing about something as Major turned the corner.

From laughter she went to a cool politeness the instant she saw him. But she was here. She had come to see him and that was good enough. Now he would have a chance to find out what was fretting her.

"Since you're here, and since I've got an extra hammer, you may as well get down and give us a hand," Major said.

Polly acted as if she thought he was serious. "No thanks. I'm on my way to see Mr. Shepler." She turned her pony. "Good-bye, Mr. Jordan. It was nice talking to you."

She rode past Major and went across the yard at a fast trot. Major watched her on the meadow road, her dark hair shining in the morning sun.

What had been so funny to make her and Jordan laugh? Major would not ask, and Jordan was hard at work again. They talked to each other no more than necessary that day.

The following morning would be soon enough

to go see Goodwin, Major figured. In the mean-time, O'Neal and Calf Runner should be back from hunting, and Major would make very sure of the Ute's information.

As it turned out, Major did not have to make the long ride to the store. Goodwin came by late that afternoon on his way upriver on business. Major told him what Calf Runner had said about the Martins.

Goodwin did not seem surprised. "You and Jordan, the Indian, O'Neal, and Miami—and now me." He shook his head. "Don't bother to ask Calf Runner again. If he said it, it's so."

"You don't act like you're much startled."

"Burnine has been talking to me," Goodwin said quietly. "He's put a few things together, and they add up to just what Calf Runner said, and more."

"He thinks the Martins killed Sherman?"

"Perhaps. Remember this, though, there's no evidence to that effect at all. Even Burnine admits that."

"Then what do we do?"

Goodwin looked at the mountains for several moments. "Suppose we have Bill Gifford look into it."

"Gifford! What the hell! Why, he—"

"I know how you feel about him, Major, but he's the sheriff. If we don't follow lawful process, we'll backslide into anarchy again. I think we're making a little progress." Goodwin paused. "Do you want to have something done about Calf Runner's story?"

"Yes!"

"All right, but remember this, the same night Toby's house was burned, Toby was with a bunch of vigilantes burning other people's houses, and—"

"But the Martins were just hell-raising on nobody's side!" Major protested.

"I know, but it isn't much of a legal point." Goodwin frowned, studying the mountains again. "Do you want to tell Toby, and have him call on the Martins?"

"No."

"Burnine? Shall we send him?"

"He'd hang them, if he could."

Goodwin nodded. "Then it's Gifford?"

"If he spreads the story all over the country, then hell will come unhinged for sure."

"He'll keep it to himself," Goodwin said. I'll explain things to him myself. We don't know that the Martins killed Tad Sherman, and a burned house isn't enough to get the war started again. Gifford won't get any admission from the Martins, I'm sure, but his questioning of them may scare them out of doing anything more."

"Maybe," Major growled. Reluctantly he had to agree with Goodwin. "You'll see Gifford then?"

"Probably tonight. I'll swear him to silence."

Gifford could be quiet when he wanted to, Major thought. The sonofabitch had plenty of practice keeping silent about the things he had done.

Major said, "Did Ma have anything to do with getting you to send Lafait to Denver?"

Goodwin smiled and nodded. "I suppose you realize that Lafait's name is a shield protecting you to a large extent, even when he isn't here."

That was a real polite way of saying it, Major thought.

During the long and frequent absences of their husbands, Fiona and Alethea Martin found solace in talking about their days as girls back home. They told each other the same stories repeatedly. They sang hymns together. They talked about their aching, rotting teeth and wondered if the doctor they had heard was now in the country would someday wander up their way.

They each had a Spanish moidore their grandfather had given them when they were young. Through all the bad times they had managed to keep the pieces, unbeknownst to their husbands. They agreed if the doctor some day came riding up their way, they would see if he would pull the worst of their aching teeth for the coins.

Of course Spanish money was not worth much, but doctors were kind-hearted.

Their sessions together always wound up in prayer, disjointed prayer it was, in which they asked for nothing, but loudly repeated the scraps of things they remembered from revival meetings.

Alethea quite often went right on shouting the words when she was alone.

There was one great blessing at the Martin cabins: the marriages had produced no children.

This day Fiona, whose home was to the east of Alethea's, saw the horseman coming up the narrow valley. Eben and Uriah were somewhere out by the barn. She ran to get her sister and soon they were both in Fiona's cabin. "Do you suppose it's the doctor, Alethea?"

"I think it is, sister."

"How will we know?"

"We'll ask him," Alethea said boldly. "I knew he'd come this way sooner or later."

The thought of asking questions of anyone who came to see their husbands—no one else ever came—almost unhinged Fiona. The hide was off the window. She peered out cautiously at the rider, still a quarter mile away. "He *looks* like a doctor, Alethea."

"We'll march right out there and ask him. We'll show him our money and—"

"I don't know where my coin is."

"Yes, you do too. You put it between the logs near the fireplace, remember?" Alethea said.

Fiona ran to the place. She searched frantically for a time and then began to weep. "I changed the place and now I can't remember!"

They both looked for the moidore, without success. Fiona wept louder. Deliverance from the agony of her teeth was so close, and now she had lost her coin.

"Don't cry, little sister, don't cry." Alethea put her arms around Fiona. "We'll pray, and then we'll look again. *Howl, fir tree, for the cedar is fallen . . . O ye oaks of Bashan. . . .*"

The Martins had seen and recognized Bill Gifford from a long way off. They lounged by the barn and waited for him to come on in. "What do you reckon he wants?" Eben asked.

"The weasel bastard, he wants something, sure enough. I'll do the talking."

"You always do."

Gifford came in with a pleasant smile and a cheerful greeting. The Martins didn't ask him to get down and visit, but such insults never bothered Gifford; he dismounted anyway, looking around the place with a lazy air. The wagon sitting on the grassy slope below the barn was a good one. It must have been brand-new when the Martins started west with it.

It looked like it had not been moved since they arrived. Grass was growing through the spokes.

"What do you want?" Uriah asked.

"Maybe you heard, I sold most of my horses, but I've got two good ones still for sale. You fellows have seen them." Gifford watched the Martins' eyes light up with interest.

Eben said, "How much do you—"

"Hell, we couldn't buy your horses if you was

selling them for two bits a dozen," Uriah said. "Try Burnine or some other rich bastard."

Gifford looked at the sky. "Why, you just might be surprised at how cheap I can let those horses go."

"Not interested," Uriah said.

"Scarcely a cloud up there," Gifford said. "We've hardly had an all-night rain since Sherman was killed."

Uriah stared at him coldly, but Eben—that Eben was the one to watch—glanced quickly at his brother before returning his gaze to Gifford.

"Still, this is generally a good month for rain," Gifford said.

"Is it?" Uriah asked.

"I'll bet you boys that within two weeks we'll have another one of those all-night soakers. Funny thing, you know Major Whitlock has been talking some of making a dam on Deer Creek and ditching around to the mesa south of his place.

"This don't seem like a country worth going to all that trouble, considering what little you can raise. If we get our usual rain, he just might not need that ditch, wouldn't you say?"

"We wouldn't have the least idea about that," Uriah said.

Gifford got on his horse. "I'm in no busting hurry to sell those two horses. You boys take another look at them sometime when you're up my way." He turned his mount, then stopped to say something else, and then he tensed suddenly, staring with a shocked expression at the two women who appeared at the corner of the barn. They were grinning at him, snaggly-toothed grins in faces pale as a maggot. Gray streaked hair skinned tight to the head and caught in a big knot. Skinny women in filthy dresses that hung in tattered edges just above their bare feet.

It was not easy to give Bill Gifford a start, but those women did it. He recovered fast, nodded to them with a smile and removed his hat. "How do you do, ladies?"

"Are you the doctor?" one of them asked.

"Why, no, ma'am, I'm just—"

"He ain't no doctor, Alethea," Uriah said. "You damn fool women get back in the house where you belong."

"We thought. . . . He looked so nice and all—"

"Get to hell out of here!" Uriah said.

"I can tell the doctor to come up, if you ladies—"

"They don't need no doctor, goddamn it! Fool women, they get a little toothache and think they're dying. Me and Eben said we'd pull any teeth that needed pulling, but do you think they'd listen to us? No, they got to have a fancy doctor."

The women stared at Gifford with childlike appeal. "Are you sure you ain't the doctor, sir?"

"He ain't no doctor!" Eben yelled. "You heard what he said."

"He is so!" Fiona cried. "You're lying, Eben Martin." She began to weep. Her sister tried to comfort her.

Gifford rode away to a mixture of wailing and cursing. Jesus Christ! What if a man came around a sharp turn in a trail on a bright moonlight night and saw those two hags standing before him. That would be enough to put his hair on end.

Gifford set the pathetic women out of his mind entirely and reviewed his talk with the Martin brothers. Uriah had got the idea. What he would do with it was something else, so all Gifford could do was to wait and see.

You just couldn't tell which way an evil mind would veer.

Eben and Uriah watched Gifford ride away while they listened to the loud praying of their wives, now back in Fiona's cabin. Uriah sighed, "I don't know which is worse, having a snake like him come around, or having to hear those crazy women howl."

"He knows."

"He's guessed pretty good, yes."

"Shall we—"

"No, we won't!" Uriah said. "There just ain't enough people in this country for us to be free and loose the way we used to be. He ain't going to do anything."

"I ain't so sure."

"A crooked sheriff?" Uriah laughed. "Them's

the best kind, brother, real handy to have around. You know what he wants?"

"Sure. If we go shoot Major Whitlock, he gives us the two horses." Eben nodded. "Those are pretty fair horses, Uriah."

"So they are, but that ain't what I'm talking about. What he figures is having us roll Whitlock in the mud some nice rainy night so he'll have a chance to grab a chunk of Deer Valley. Them Pilcher brats of Whitlock's would drift away like smoke, once Whitlock was gone.

"Same with Jordan. Same with O'Neal and that little Indian bastard that shadows him." Uriah spat. "That Gifford thinks he's smart and greasy slick."

A warm, slow spreading excitement had grown in Eben. People just didn't know about all the planning, all the cautious looking-over it took to make a real good job of killing. They thought it was just a matter of blundering up to a place and pulling a trigger. "Are we going to do it, brother?" he asked.

"No, by God!"

"Why not?"

"One good reason, that goddamn murdering brother of Whitlock's. I know his kind. He'd follow us to hell and gone."

"He'd never know," Eben said.

"You fool, don't you think Gifford wouldn't work it out so that he did know?"

"Then we ought to get the brother first. Some good rainy night when—"

"I said no! We went just a mite too far, maybe, when I let you plunk old Sherman. We ain't doing nothing more until things flare up again real good."

Chapter Fourteen

Frank Millar was scared clear down to the bottom of his broken boots when the two riders caught him red-handed beside the dead yearling steer. He was a blonde young man in a ragged Union blouse, a prospector whose search had been most discouraging. About everything had run out for him, and now it looked like he himself was done.

Burnine and his foreman, Harry Culwell, sat their horses and looked at Millar, Culwell waiting for orders and Burnine doing some quick, hard thinking.

Their silence made it all the worse for Millar. He pointed with his bloody knife at the steer. "Yours?" he gulped.

"Where'd you come from?" Burnine asked.

"Indiana. I—"

"I mean recently, damn it!"

"I was in the San Luis Valley and I was headed for the San Juans, but there was an Indian scare, so I—"

"You ever been in this country before?" Burnine demanded.

"No, sir. I'm no thief. I couldn't find a deer and I had only one powder charge left, and I was hungry. I'll pay you. I'll work it out—"

"We hang people around here for what you've done," Burnine said quietly.

Looking at the two of them, Millar believed it.

Then Burnine said, "You go on up to the camp, Culwell. I'll be along in a few minutes."

Burnine made his deal with Millar. When he rode into cow camp a half hour later with Millar, Burnine told his foreman to keep his mouth shut about the fact that Millar was going to stay there for a while.

There had been enough general meetings, enough wrangling about plans to handle the Regulators. The lull since the Big Fire Raid and Sherman's death had been Burnine's idea; let the Regulators think they had made their point, that nothing was going to happen.

Something was going to happen, but it would come about as a result of Burnine's planning, and now he thought he had it worked out.

Five days later, when they rode to hang Brent Lavington, no one but Burnine knew the full extent of the plans.

Separately and by different routes Toby and Jake McAllister went to join Burnine three miles north of his place on the old buffalo trail. Shad knew nothing about it; he didn't count any more.

Jake asked some questions and Burnine said, "Just come along and find out." He looked at his big silver watch. He was a great one for having things timed just right, Burnine was.

They met Culwell, waiting in a pinon gulch, two miles farther north. Burnine checked his watch again. "How was Millar when he left you?"

"All right," Culwell said. "Kind of scared, but he'll do it, I'm certain."

"What the hell is all the secrecy about?" Jake protested.

"So we don't have a bungled mess like the last time." Burnine gave detailed orders about how to approach Kettle Drum Springs. Only he would use the trail. Even then he did not tell them that the Pilchers were coming in from the north, also on a strict time schedule.

"Suppose he ain't home?" Jake asked.

"He's home. His boys are off in the hills some-where. His wife and daughter are at the Sherman place, taking care of the garden. Unless they change their habits, they won't be back till noon."

Jake eyed Burnine with new respect. He got out a gold watch he had borrowed from his father. "I've got eight-twenty."

"It's running right with mine then. Be where I told you before ten-thirty. At ten-thirty you'll hear a shot. That's the signal. We'll go in, do the job, and be gone in fifteen minutes."

"Are we afraid of him, or something?" Jake asked.

Burnine gave him a cold look. "Yes. He's on edge. He's been keeping lookout like a pirate. Unless we want to get him like bushwhackers, we could lose a couple of men."

They scattered toward their assigned positions. Toby and Jake were together for a short distance. "That Burnine . . ." Jake shook his head. "What's the difference how we get rid of Lavington?"

"Hanging is law, in a way. Just shooting a man from cover is murder." Toby looked doubtful of his own words. "I guess that's the way Burnine sees it."

Brent Lavington heard the horses coming, He grabbed his rifle from where it lay close to the harness he was mending and ran into the trees uphill from the cabin. His position in the pit at the base of an uprooted yellow pine tree commanded a lot of ground.

Straight ahead, the valley leading down to the Sherman place was open ground. Choppy, plunging hills flanked it on both sides, extremely poor ground for horsemen, except where the trail came through saddles at the head of the valley. The weakness of Lavington's position was the timber at his back.

He rested his rifle on a tree root and waited.

It flashed through his mind that this was a miserable existence. Though it would tear his pride to run, it might be that he would come to that in time. At least he could then have a full night of unbroken sleep.

The man was taking a long time getting over that last hill to the south, but when he came into sight, leading his horse, Lavington felt a little better. The animal was limping on its right foreleg. A small packhorse with prospecting tools.

Lavington sized the man up quickly, a ragged fellow in a faded and torn Union blouse. He had never seen him before, but he did not accept him at face value just because of that fact. He stayed where he was and kept his rifle ready.

"Hello, the cabin!" the visitor shouted as he came down the hill. He pulled the packhorse away when it tried to wade in at the upper end of the spring to drink, and led it on around to the overflow. Once more he hailed the cabin.

For a while Lavington paid him no attention. He studied the trail, the valley, and the crests of the rough hills.

All was quiet, normal.

Lavington felt hellish tired all of a sudden. He wondered how much longer he could go on, distrusting every sound, every natural movement around the springs, every stranger who came by.

The horse drank its fill and then raised its head

to watch Lavington's two horses in the corral. Its owner led it out of the stream and examined its foreleg, shaking his head worriedly. Lavington crawled out of the pit and went down the hill, making no sound until he left the needle mat under the trees and struck hard ground below.

His approach startled the man. "I didn't think there was anybody home. I yelled a time or two but—"

"Where'd you come from?"

Millar pointed south. "That big valley over there—the San Luis."

"When?" Lavington glanced at a muzzle loading carbine lashed on top the pack.

"What's the idea of the questions, mister?"

"How long have you been in this country?"

For a moment Millar acted like he was going to turn angry, and then he shrugged. "This is my second day. If you don't mind, I'll get on as fast as my horse can limp."

He had no pistol, Lavington was sure. He seemed to be just what he appeared to be, a wandering, down-on-his-luck prospector. They were scratching at the hills everywhere these days. "How long has that horse been limping?"

"Not very long." Millar stepped over to the stream, squatting, cupping his hands to drink.

Lavington still was taking no chances. He put his rifle down close to hand before he lifted the foreleg of the horse. Why, there was a rock jammed in the hoof—he dropped the leg and reached for his rifle.

He was too late. Millar had swung around and was covering him with a two-barrelled derringer.

"I don't want to hurt you, Mr. Lavington." Millar's voice trembled a little. The big-bored, ugly weapon was not quite steady in his hand either, but firm enough, considering the distance between them.

"Who sent you?" Lavington looked at the saddle where the trail came from the south. He had no doubts about who had sent the man.

Millar came closer. "All they wanted was not to get anybody hurt when they came to take you in for a fair trial." His expression was so honest and apologetic that Lavington thought he probably did believe what he was saying.

"Kick that rifle off to the side."

Lavington put his foot close to the rifle. It lay on uneven ground. He worked his foot until the toe of the boot went under the weapon just ahead of the back sight. "Look, I'll go in with you, if that's all you want."

Millar took a small watch from his pocket. He flipped the case open with a broken thumbnail. "I had to do this, Mr. Lavington. If I had time to explain, you could see why." His eyes kept flicking from Lavington to the watch. "Well, I reckon . . ."

He snapped the case lid shut and raised the derringer to fire a shot overhead.

Lavington's timing was not all that it might have been. The rifle wobbled as he flipped it up with his toe and his catch was clumsy. Millar brought the derringer down to cover him again and had his attitude been set on killing, he could have done it, but for just a thin slice of time he hesitated.

And then the rifle thumped against the side of his head, the impact slightly broken by the floppy brim of his slouch hat. The derringer dropped from his hand unfired and he fell senseless to the ground.

They would be crowding hard to hear that signal shot, Lavington knew. It might already be too late. He expected time to end for him every second while he was saddling a horse.

He had five minutes but he didn't know that. Burnine's orders were to wait that long if the signal did not come exactly on time.

In less than four minutes he was out of sight, around the base of Castle Hill, over the steep crest of the first rise and into the nightmare of heavy up and down going where a rider would go only in a great emergency.

Matt Pilcher came out of the timber on foot and saw Millar on hands and knees near the spring, trying to get up. Matt was the first. All the others closed in a minute or two afterward.

As usual when a plan had blown up, Burnine was cold and steady. He didn't even bother to ask Millar what had happened, after he found out that

Millar didn't know which way Lavington had run.

"Hey! Here's a woman's watch," Matt said, picking up the timepiece.

Burnine plucked it from his fingers and put it away with a look that forbade any request for an explanation.

They picked up Lavington's trail quickly. "He'll kill his horse, going at that rate through those hills," Culwell said.

"If he intends to go all the way through them," Burnine mused. "Jake, you and Toby stay with his tracks. Culwell, you take Matt and Mark and go down to the valley road. Don't let him break south, whatever you do. The rest of us will take the buffalo trail."

Millar staggered over to Burnine. "I could have shot him, but—" From the contemptuous expressions around him he realized that there was much more to this than the matter of taking in a man for trial.

He held the derringer toward Burnine. "Here, take it back."

"Keep it. Let's call it your pay."

"I don't want it," Millar said sullenly. A sneak's weapon. A sneak's trick too. All that talk he'd believed about being hanged for killing a steer. What a fool he'd been.

"You keep it, Millar," Burnine said. "Maybe you can make a sugar titty out of it. You need one."

They laughed and rode away.

•••

Brent Lavington didn't kill his horse going through the choppy hills—not quite, but it didn't have much left when he came down the last steep slope close to where Chunk and Burt Pilcher were loading clay into a wagon. "Is there a good horse at Major's?" he shouted.

"Up in the field!" Chunk yelled.

Before he got across the mesa, Lavington saw them coming, three who had skirted the eastern end of the hills, and three more galloping down from the buffalo trail. His horse was wobbling but it took itself on heart across the mesa and down the hill to Major's cabin.

Lavington had hoped that Major would be there, with his horse handy, but there was no one around. He fell as he tried to dismount running, and then he scrambled up and ran down to the edge of the meadow. He saw two horses, upstream, about a quarter mile away.

If his own horse had just enough left . . . but it did not. It was standing spraddle-legged, head down with a rope of froth hanging from its muzzle.

On the crest of the hill a man yelled and then a bullet struck the sod close to Lavington's feet and he heard the boom of a rifle. He put the cabin between himself and the rider up there as he ran, back to the building, and then around the corner to plunge through the doorway.

Even in desperation his mind took note of the fact that Major had put a board floor in the place.

Major heard the rifle shot but he had no time to give it much thought, for O'Neal, pitching violently with fever on his buffalo robes in his cottonwood shanty, was about all Major could pay attention to at the moment. Two hours before Miami had come to him for help and he had been with O'Neal ever since, after sending Miami to get Ma.

"Shoot low, you thieving bastards!" O'Neal yelled, and whaled around with fists like pinon knots.

With a horn spoon Major dipped water from a skillet and dribbled it into the sick man's mouth. And then O'Neal knocked the skillet out of his hands.

There were two more shots, not nearly as loud as the first one. Maybe Chunk and Burt were trying out that new pistol again, shooting at prairie dogs as they hauled clay to the ditch on the south mesa.

Both shots had come from Major's cabin. The first one killed the horse as it stood trying to brace itself against death. Lavington's second shot came from high in the wall where he had knocked out chinking where the logs were not covered by the addition.

The second shot, whizzed close to Ross Pilcher,

who was standing with a group at the edge of the mesa. They fell back quickly and Ross said, "He means business!"

"What the hell do you think we mean?" Burnine rasped. The very thing he had wanted to avoid had happened again. They had to go against a stout cabin. Already he could see indecision on the faces of the Pilchers. Jake McAllister and Culwell were the only ones he could trust to go all the way without whining.

"We've started, and this time we're going through with it." Burnine put a hard look on the Pilchers.

Jake and Toby were still back in the broken hills somewhere, laboring along on Lavington's trail.

Burnine knew that if he allowed his bunch much time to think, they would remember too well what had happened at William Grosland's cabin on Little Creek one night. He gave orders calculated to keep everyone busy.

Matt and Mark relished their assignment. They rode back across the mesa and met their half brothers coming toward the ditch with a load of clay. Before Chunk and Burt knew what was happening, Matt and Mark were pointing pistols at them. Only Burt was armed. He obeyed the order and tossed his pistol on the clay near the endgate of the wagon.

Matt scooped it up. "Well, a brand-new six-shooter! I'll just make a trade with you, Burt, for my old one. That is, if you behave yourself like we tell you."

"Like hell you will!" Burt cried.

Mark leaned close and rapped him on the head with the barrel of his pistol. "Mind your manners, brother."

"Where's O'Neal and that Indian brat?" Matt demanded.

"In the hills." Chunk thought he was telling the truth.

"Where's old Maje, the big man?"

Chunk shook his head.

Mark rapped him with his pistol. "Speak up, brother."

"I don't know. And I'm no brother of yours, you sonofabitch!"

"They need a lesson, Mark," Matt said. "Running off from home like they done has made them awful disrespecting." He began to uncoil his rope.

"You hit one of us with that and by God I'll kill you!" Chunk yelled.

"What a way to talk. *Tck, tck!*" Matt measured out the rope.

"Lay off that kind of stuff," Mark said. "We don't— Hey! Here comes the McAllisters."

Matt recoiled the rope. "I was only funning."

Chunk and Burt looked at each other. *Like hell,* their expressions said.

Jake and Toby McAllister were hot and disgusted. Not knowing Lavington's intentions, they had trailed him cautiously, but even so, their horses were badly worn. "You got him, huh?" Jake said.

"We will," Matt answered. "We got him trapped in Major's cabin."

"Where's Major?" Toby asked quickly.

"We don't know." Matt jerked his thumb toward his half brothers. "They claim they don't know either."

Chunk said quietly, "You may be lucky, Catfish Mouth, if you don't find him."

"We don't have to look," Mark said. "What could old Maje do if he showed up?"

"He could get the Sheplers down here, that's what he could do!" Matt yelled angrily. "Christ awmighty, didn't you listen to anything Burnine said? What do you think he sent Culwell to round up Jordan for, and us to get these traitorous little brats?"

The McAllisters started to ride on.

"Wait a minute!" Matt shouted. "You've got to take Chunk and Burt to their cabin and guard 'em."

"Who says?" Jake demanded.

"Burnine, that's who. For once, we want something to go right."

Major ran to the doorway when he heard the hoofs. It was too soon for Miami to be returning with Ma, but he was willing to welcome help from anyone. "Oh, you two," he said disgustedly when he saw Matt and Mark Pilcher. He turned back to O'Neal.

He didn't look around again until the Pilchers blocked the light in the low doorway. They were pointing pistols at him. "You crazy, or something?" he asked, struggling to keep O'Neal from getting up.

"Come on out of there," Matt ordered.

"I've got a sick man here, you fool!"

"He's been sick before. Get up from there and come out."

"Go to hell."

Matt cocked his pistol. "You heard what I said."

Holding O'Neal's arms as the man groaned and heaved and scissored his legs, Major didn't look at Matt when he said, "Go ahead, you cowardly sonofabitch, shoot me."

"Look, Matt, the old man really is sick. You can tell—" Mark said.

"Shut up! First, those snot-nosed half brothers of yours cussing me, and now Major, and you standing there telling me what to do." Matt took his frustration out on his brother, and then he said, "Get those guns."

With one eye on Major, Mark gathered up O'Neal's eight-sider, and the rifle gun Lavington had given to Miami. Major couldn't keep from saying, "Lafait had to come for that Sharps once."

"Lafait is a long ways from here now," Matt blustered.

The Pilchers went outside and held a low-voiced conference. Suddenly, Mark stuck his head in the doorway. "You got a pistol with you, Major?"

O'Neal had quieted down. Major rose to stretch his legs, and cracked his head on the low ridge-log. "If I had a pistol, Matt would likely be dead now!" He staggered outside and blinked at the brightness. "What's got into you two?"

"Brent Lavington is holed up in your cabin," Matt said. "His time is come, and we're going to see to it."

"In my—!" Major saw a small group of men near the edge of the mesa, and beyond them, the wagon. "Who—" He stared. "Why, that's Toby's horse up there by the wagon."

"You see good." Matt got on his horse. "I've decided to let you stay here. Shoot him in the guts, Mark, if he tries to get funny." Matt laughed. "Yep, we got Lavington right where we want him. We'll likely have to burn the place to get him out of there, but hell, it won't be the first cabin that's been burned, including those of ours." He rode away.

Major was so cold with anger that he mumbled when he said, "Anybody burns my place, I'll kill every one of them."

Mark eyed him warily, awed. "You're talking about your own brother-in-law, and Burnine, and a few others."

O'Neal began to rave again. Major went back

into the cabin. "Easy now, easy," he said help-lessly.

"Shoot low, you thieving bastards, shoot low!"

Jordan was about ready to go back and help Chunk and Burt with the ditch work, but he stayed a few minutes longer in the cool of an aspen thicket, watching Major's young bull rubbing its neck against a tree. Jordan grinned. It was some outfit, when you could take a short ride and count every blessed head the owner had.

Well, a man had to make a start. Major was sure enough doing that. One day these thickets would be crawling with cattle and when that time came, Jordan knew that if he stuck it out, he would be a solid part of the outfit. In between would be a power of clay hauling and ditch digging and such-like, but on the whole the prospect was good enough for a man not afraid of work.

Riding down toward the south mesa, Jordan heard three shots. The first one was from a rifle gun, he was sure. The other two were not as loud, and he was not positive about whether they were rifle shots or from a pistol. Chunk and Burt were hell for wasting powder on prairie dogs.

The sounds made him uneasy. Just two days before he had found the third dead steer from Major's bunch, a carcass months old.

When he saw Harry Culwell riding toward him, he was still edgy. Culwell stopped and waited for him, and then asked, "What's the shooting about, Frank?"

"I was going to ask you the same question."

Culwell shrugged. "Beats me. I was just coming back from Pilcher Town. Mr. Burnine told me to take a look at that bull he sold Major. How's he doing?"

"He's back there about a quarter mile. Take a look at him. I'm going on in myself."

Culwell yawned. "To hell with the bull. I'll ride along with you."

They were near the upper end of the mesa before Jordan saw anything amiss. Far ahead, Major's wagon was near the break of the hill, with three or four men near it. Jordan turned toward Culwell and looked directly into the muzzle of a pistol.

"Ease your rifle out of the boot, Frank, and hand it to me."

After several moments Jordan obeyed the order.

"What do you think you're doing, Culwell?"

"I'm taking you down to Chunk's cabin. All you've got to do is stay there. You'll have company."

Jordan gauged the distance to the edge of the mesa. He knew Culwell pretty well. Maybe the man wouldn't shoot him if he made a run for it. "What's going on?" He kneed his horse lightly to turn it.

"Brent Lavington is holed up in Major's cabin." Culwell raised the rifle a little. "Don't try that,

216

Jordan. I'll kill your horse if you do, and walk you on down to that cabin."

He would, too, Jordan realized glumly. "You're going to try to get him out of there and hang him?"

"Yes."

"You for that, Culwell?"

"I work for Burnine."

"Good enough for you. I work for Major, and I'll tell you here and now that if he gets hurt in this stinking deal of Burnine's, you and him and whoever else is mixed up in it will be better off if you kill me right now."

Culwell watched him sharply for a moment. He didn't doubt that Jordan meant what he said. "What's so damn special about Major Whitlock?" A hard-working, overly solemn young fellow—that seemed to be about his size, as Culwell saw it.

"He thinks decent." That covered it for Jordan.

In Major's cabin, Lavington kept watch from the loopholes he'd knocked in the chinking. He had covered the windows with their board shutters, loaded all the weapons in the place—and now he had to stand them off until help came.

They wanted him alive. They hadn't cracked a cap after that one shot.

From the new room he'd seen hulking Matt Pilcher taking cover in the cottonwoods west of the cabin.

That new room was the bad part of this. It jutted

out awkwardly beyond the connecting doorway, making a blind spot. He'd bored some holes with an auger, and he could also see through cracks in the boards that covered the rough-framing for the windows Major didn't yet have; but if he fired a shot from behind those thin walls, he'd have only inch boards between him and the return fire. He'd have to stay in the main room most of the time.

They were out to hang him. Burn him out and then shoot him in the legs, that's what they would try. They didn't know it but he had a fear of fire and smoke far greater than some men had of muddy, tumbling water in a great river. If they tried . . .

If they tried . . . That was weak self-delusion. Hell yes, they would set the place on fire. As soon as it was dark they would creep in. The boards of the new room were already dry, and the cabin logs were dry. As if it were already happening, he saw the shakes curling with flame, smoke choking him, the roof collapsing.

He broke out in a cold sweat and fought an urge to burst from the door and run for it. Instead, he went into the new room and used his peepholes. He saw no one on the hill, but he knew they were there, nor did he see anything of Matt Pilcher in the trees, but he knew he was there somewhere, waiting.

Waiting for dark. There was a horror about buildings flaming high in the night. Once when he was little, near Springfield, Illinois, he had been coining home with his parents from a prayer meeting and they had stopped the wagon in the warm, humid night to watch a farmhouse burning.

Men were running around futilely with buckets from a well. A woman, held by other women, was moaning, and from the second story of the house came the screams of children.

Lavington had been sick in bed for three days afterward, and all that summer he'd had nightmares.

He went back to the main room and made his rounds of the loopholes, and then he put the ladder up and climbed into the loft to examine it again. He bent his back and put slow pressure against the shakes on the north slope of the roof, loosening them enough until he was satisfied that he could break through with one quick surge.

They would be watching the doors and windows. When the time came he might, he just might, surprise them enough to get a running start by going out through the roof.

The wagon came from the north about a half hour later.

Lavington watched it hopefully all the way across the soft meadow road. The man had to stop twice to rest the team. A woman and several kids, settlers on their way down to Goodwin's.

When they came abreast of the cabin, he opened the door a trifle. "Don't look this way. Get

word to the Groslands. Lavington. Deer Valley."
He spoke just loud enough for the words to carry.

Of course the man looked. He stopped his team
and said, "What?" in a loud voice.

"Keep going." Lavington repeated his message,
and the driver looked all around with a scared
expression before he went on up the hill. No good,
Lavington thought, but it was the best he could do.

He was right, it was no good. Beyond the crest
of the hill, when the driver stopped to rest his
team again, a short, heavy man with blistered
cheekbones walked over to him and said, "Stop
at that cabin you see over there on the flat. Stay
there until it's safe to leave."

"What—what's going on, mister?"

"Just stop there where I told you and wait.
Understand?"

The man nodded.

Lying on his stomach at the edge of the hill,
Luke Pilcher had about enough of the hot sun on
his back. He said, "Maybe I'd best go along with
them to make sure—"

"No need," Burnine said. "He catches on. Don't
you, mister?"

The man bobbed his head. Burnine waved him
on.

They did not wait until dark. In the middle of the
afternoon Lavington saw the wagon appear at the
top of the hill, its tongue lashed back, the box

heaped with wood. He wanted to run but he fired until the gloomy room was rotten with smoke, aiming under the wagon in the hope of having a deflecting shot strike one of the men behind it; but the angle of the hill was against him.

They pushed the wagon until the back wheels were over the crest. It was poised then for its run dead at the cabin, held only by a long rope leading back to the team of oxen.

Ross Pilcher didn't like it. He hadn't figured on burning Major's place. He could remember how those Whitlock younguns had worked their hearts out to build it. Old Ross hadn't figured on a lot of things when he let his sons bully him into this try at hanging Brent Lavington.

"Mr. Burnine, I'm against this. I've been thinking maybe—"

"Shut up, Pa!" Luke snarled, and tossed a burning pinon torch into the prepared nest of dry grass and brown pine needles in the middle of the wood.

Whatever protest old Ross thought to make died soundlessly in a welter of self-pity because the Lord had seen fit to punish him with sons like Matthew, Mark and Luke. The Apostles.

The fire took hold quickly.

Lavington watched it come at him. He had emptied all the weapons in the room. He knew that he should be reloading his rifle, so that it would be ready when he ran from the cabin; but he had no will for anything but to press his face to the loophole in the powder-stinking room.

The wagon gathered speed. It struck a soft spot and veered to the right, lurching, almost turning over. It was going to miss him, it was going to miss him! The left wheel bounced against a loose rock and the wagon straightened out again, coming on course, like an evil, living thing, with smoke and flame trailing out behind it.

The exultant yells of the men lying tight against the ground at the crest of the hill became in Lavington's mind the screams of children trapped in a burning farmhouse. He could not run, or cry out. All he could do was watch.

Chapter Fifteen

As soon as he had told Mrs. Goodwin about O'Neal, Miami was in a stew to return to Deer Valley. "You get my horse out of the pasture down there, young man, and hitch up the wagon while I'm gathering up a few things here. I'll get there that much sooner then."

O'Neal said about half the trouble of the world was women giving orders, but now Miami found himself trotting to obey. Mrs. Goodwin was ready to go by the time he came up from the Little Creek pasture with her horse. She helped him hitch up and then she said, "Stop twisting and get on back, and then keep right on going to Alamaba

Crossing to find Dr. Kimball. It would be a miracle if you found him home, so—"

"Yes, ma'am. I know some of the cricks where he prospects. I'll find him." Miami rode away. He tried to remember everything O'Neal had told him about covering a lot of ground without killing a horse by hurrying. He treated O'Neal's gray horse with respect, but he kept him moving too. At Chico Brush he let him water. After that Miami left the road and headed toward the old Indian trail near the river. It was much shorter, if you didn't get lost in the rocks.

Miami did not get lost. He arrived at the cottonwoods at the lower end of Deer Creek in good time. Suppose O'Neal had died while he was gone? Please God, no. Miami Rusk didn't look much like the Angry One then; he was just a scared youngun.

Calf Runner stepped out from behind a tree and signalled for him to stop. Miami didn't have time to visit. He shook his head, made the sick sign, and pointed toward O'Neal's cabin.

"No!" Calf Runner ordered. His hands cut the air in quick sign language. Bad one there. One of the bad ones with the sunset in his hair, the Rojo.

Miami turned back to Calf Runner. The Ute told the story as he chose to interpret what he had seen. Two of the bad red-haired ones had come to O'Neal's lodge. They quarrelled with Major. One had gone away. The other was still there, on guard. They wanted O'Neal to die, and Major too. The guard would keep all help away. Then Major would catch the fever from O'Neal and both would die. Calf Runner had been waiting. Calf Runner knew that O'Neal's son, the Angry One, would do something.

Mark Pilcher was tired of standing guard at the cabin. All the fun was up there on the mesa, where they were getting ready to burn Lavington out. He'd tried to make Major feel bad about it, losing his house, with that nice big new room and all, but it hadn't turned out the way Mark figured.

Major just gave him a long, thoughty look that reminded Mark of Lafait. Some folks—Gifford was one of them—said that Major was a damn sight more dangerous and cold-blooded than Lafait ever thought of being.

Mark didn't say any more about Major losing his cabin.

How had all this trouble and fighting come about anyway? Mark remembered when him and Major had been good friends, when they were younguns crossing the plains. Why, he used to fun Major about that red-headed girl he was so soft on, and old Maje would get all solemn and silly looking and then he would grin sheeplike and say, "Aw, you shut up, Markus Barkus."

Well, things had changed. There was your old answer, things had just naturally changed.

Mark made another trip around the little cabin. He wasn't going to take no chances of somebody sneaking in on him across the open ground if he stayed too long in one spot.

Then he saw the Indian walk out of the cottonwoods at the foot of the hill. Mark didn't think much of Indians, but this one was unarmed, just moseying along the edge of the meadow like he'd lost something there. All at once he made a big dive into the tall grass. He grabbed something and it looked like a hell of a struggle, but when he got up, the thing he'd been tussling with had got away.

A mouse? Mark had heard that they ate mice, but Jesus, a mouse couldn't put up no fight like that. The Indian began to sneak up on another one, whatever it was. He dived on it and there was an awful fracas of rolling and thrashing around. But again it got away.

Mark was completely absorbed.

He never heard the faintest sound from Miami Rusk until an instant before Miami came around the corner of the cabin and hit him in the back of the head with an Arapaho war club borrowed from Calf Runner.

Major didn't know what had happened, either, until Miami bounded through the doorway and asked, "Is he—? How is he?"

"About the same. A little quieter right now. Did you find my ma?"

"She's coming." Miami watched the heave and fall of O'Neal's chest for a moment. "I'm going after the doctor."

"No use, Miami. He—"

"I'm going after him!" All of Miami's wild hatred of Major came to his face in an instant.

It sort of shocked Major; it always would, but he held his temper and said quietly, "Dr. Kimball came by yesterday when I was working on the ditch. He said he was going gold hunting up some gulch near Granite." He shook his head. "You couldn't find him in time to do O'Neal any good. He'll be on his feet before you could even get to wherever Kimball went."

"You're lying!"

Major took a deep breath. "How'd you get in here? What—" He jumped up and went to the door and saw Mark lying on the ground. "You killed him!"

"All right, I killed him!"

Hell's lava would spill over now, Major thought bitterly; but it was running anyway. "Drag him behind the cabin. Put on his hat and coat and stand around outside so they won't get suspicious."

"Who's they?"

Major explained what was happening at his cabin. "Now go get Mark out of sight."

Directly, he heard Miami grunting as he dragged Mark around to the back of the cabin. "His old hat don't fit," Miami called.

"Wear it anyway. Have they been looking this way?"

"Naw! They're busy with a wagon. . . . They're . . ." Miami didn't finish then. A few minutes later he came rushing to the door and cried, "We got to do something to help Lavington! They got a wagonload of wood and they're going to push it down—"

"What do you think we can do?" Major asked savagely.

Miami looked abashed before the sudden outburst. "Well, something."

"Sure! I can try something, if you stay here and take care of O'Neal, but when I show up over there, they'll wonder how I got away from Mark. Somebody will come over here to see—and then what, Miami?"

Miami backed away from the door. "I don't think I meant to kill him."

"No, no! Nobody means to kill nobody, but it comes about just the same, and now the whole stinking mess has fallen smack into my valley!"

"Don't act like I started it."

A little later Major heard the muffled sound of Lavington's frantic shooting, and Miami yelled, "They've set the wagon on fire!"

O'Neal bellered his favorite advice about shooting low, and then he thrashed around and accused somebody of stealing his horse. Major had just got him quieted when Mark Pilcher came stumbling in, with Miami driving him at pistol point. "He ain't dead after all!"

"I can see," Major growled. It was the first good thing that had happened all day. With his mouth hanging loose, Mark staggered over to a corner and sat down, holding his head. Major gave him a cup of water and he drank greedily.

"Gawd! My neck hurts something awful. What happened?"

"I told you I didn't aim to kill him," Miami said.

Brent Lavington watched the old nightmare come at him, only this time it was real, and his mind was thirty-five years in the past, back at the flaming farmhouse where the children had appeared once at the second-floor window, smoke-misty faces crying through the crimson night.

I've got to jump, Lavington told himself; I've got to jump to the ground and run. But he couldn't move to help himself.

It ended but the nightmare ran on. The weakness of the wheel the Whitlocks had repaired on the very ground where the cabin now stood saved Lavington. The wagon bounced over a rock and the spokes popped loose. The wheel crumpled, the axle dug in, slewing the wagon around. It dumped over sidewise, spilling its burning cargo down the gravelly slope.

Even after the threat was gone, Lavington could not move for a while, but when the inertia of terror left him, he went to work swiftly reloading the weapons on the floor around him.

Matt Pilcher grew careless as he tried to crawl in closer to the cabin. Lavington fired through an auger hole at him. The opening was not large enough for accurate aiming but the shot was close enough to drive Matt back, and that gave Lavington time to run into the main room.

Matt began to fire into the addition.

"Stop that shooting!" Burnine yelled. They would wait. They would let the inaction bear on Lavington. A man busy defending himself had little time to think, but a man wondering about the silence and the next move of his enemies might crack and make a run for it.

If Lavington tried to run, he wouldn't have a chance.

Burnine told Toby McAllister to go relieve his brother guarding the hostages in Chunk's cabin. "Tell Jake to get over here."

"What are we going to do, just wait around?" Luke Pilcher asked.

"Yep," Burnine said.

Old Ross was nervous. "That'll give time for the Sheplers or maybe the south-end bunch to get here."

"Maybe." Burnine gave him a cold look. "Who's going to tell them?"

"Polly Lavington."

Burnine shook his head. "She can't hear rifle

shots from here to Kettle Drum Springs. Sure, she's probably found her father gone by now, but that won't mean too much.

"Millar is loose too, but he's had all the trouble he wants. I don't think he'll stop before he gets to the mines. We'll wait."

Burnine squinted across the valley at O'Neal's cabin. He did not see Mark on guard but he knew he must be doing his part, since Major had not shown up. That was good. Burnine didn't want anything to happen to Major if it could be helped.

Burnine sat down in the shade of his horse to wait. Though the others did not like his plan of waiting, no one argued until Jake McAllister showed up. Jake wanted action immediately. "He may sneak out of there and—"

"Hope he does," Burnine said. "Keep an eye on the west end of that grove. If he comes out, he'll run for those horses in the valley. We can overtake him and rope him long before he makes it."

Jake was for burning the cabin to get Lavington out.

"Not unless we have to," Burnine said.

Hours later Mrs. Goodwin came by in her light spring wagon. Burnine's group touched their hats and spoke respectfully to her. She told them why she was there.

"How'd you know about the sick man?" Burnine asked.

"Miami Rusk brought me word."

Burnine nodded pleasantly. "I see."

"What's going on?"

"Nothing important, ma'am." Burnine looked at Culwell. "Crawl over to the hill and yell down to him so Mrs. Goodwin can go past."

Culwell called Lavington by name, so by the time Mrs. Goodwin drove down the hill, she had guessed the situation fairly well. As she went past Major's cabin, Lavington spoke to her from one of his loopholes. "Try to get word to the Sheplers."

The woman nodded slightly to show that she had heard, but, knowing Burnine, she doubted that she would have a chance to send word up the river.

She was right. As soon as she left the mesa, Burnine told Culwell, "Get over to O'Neal's cabin. See about that Rusk brat. Wait till Mrs. Goodwin gets there and then bring Major back and put him with the others."

"And if the Rusk kid ain't there?"

"Then he ain't there, that's all!"

And if he wasn't, the Sheplers would be along in time to turn this thing into a deadly fight, Culwell thought. He went to follow orders, along the mesa and across the lower valley.

Miami was not at O'Neal's cabin. Mark Pilcher was still there, all right, lying in the corner with all the fight out of him. The only reason Culwell bothered to ask about what had happened to him was because he had to report back to Burnine.

"He hit his head on the ridgelog," Major said. "You can see how low it is."

"Yeah. Where's Miami Rusk?"

"He went after Dr. Kimball."

"Sure. By way of the Shepler places, I suppose?"

Major shook his head. "That would make it hot for you, wouldn't it?"

Culwell looked at Mark. "What happened to you?"

"Miami hit me with a rifle barrel, I guess."

"You guess?" Culwell said disgustedly. He tried again. "Where's Miami now?"

"Major sent him after the doctor."

"Where is the doctor?"

"Somewhere around Granite." Mark was in no condition to know or care about details. He knew what he had heard Major tell the Indian brat when they were talking outside the cabin. What he hadn't heard wasn't bothering him, so now he confirmed what Major had wanted him to overhear. "All I know is he said for Miami to ride like hell and not to stop nowhere."

"How long ago?"

"Two hours, maybe three—I don't know. Christ, I think my skull is busted and you stand there asking questions."

Culwell knew he was not going to get any satisfactory answers from either one of them. All he could do was tell Burnine and let him make the decisions.

"Your ma will be here pretty quick, Major. Then you're going with me."

"Good! I want to talk to Burnine."

"You'd better go back with me too, Mark," Culwell said.

Mark shook his head, and then he grabbed the back of his neck and groaned. Pilchers, Culwell thought; the whole goddamn bunch wasn't worth shooting.

Mrs. Goodwin arrived not long afterward. Culwell helped her and Major bundle O'Neal up in clean blankets. She expressed her fury by hurling the buffalo robes toward the door. They struck Culwell and for a moment he was tangled up and Major could have jumped him, but Major only picked the robes up and carried them outside. "I've got to go now, Ma, but—"

"Shoot low, you thieving bastards!" O'Neal yelled.

"Same old tune," Ma said. "Did Miami go for the doctor?"

"Yes," Major lied.

Ma glanced at Mark. "What ails *him?*"

"Headache where his guts ought to be," Culwell said. "Let's go."

The Smoke horse had wandered off. Major didn't care. After the long hours in the cramped cabin, he was glad to walk. They crossed the lower meadows and went up the hill. Jake McAllister was lying with his rifle north of the badger diggings where Miami once had hidden.

Culwell asked, "Where's Mr. Burnine?"

"Somewhere in the trees behind the cabin." Jake lifted on his elbows and looked behind him. "I might have known," he growled. "He got it out of Bessie."

Shad McAllister was pounding up the road on a tired horse. Rage was written all over his face when he rode over to the three men. "So you're at it again, you and Burnine!" he roared at Culwell.

"I'm only following orders, Mr. McAllister."

Shad cursed, glaring at Jake. "Orders! I gave Jake and Toby orders too, and then they sneaked off to hang a man. Where's Toby?"

"At Chunk's cabin," Jake said sullenly.

"Lavington is trapped in my place," Major said. "Before someone gets killed, I want to go down there and talk to him. If I can get him to come out, will you and Burnine promise to let us take him to Denver for a trial?"

"Hell yes!" Shad yelled. And then he added. "What are you going to try him for?"

"For whatever these people are wanting to kill him for now," Major said.

"That's a dirty trick!" Jake shouted. "There ain't nothing against him." He realized what he had said and added lamely, "Legal-like, that is."

"You shut up," Shad said. "You go down there,

Major. If you can stop this murdering business, I'll ride with Lavington myself as far as the Sheplers."

"You can't promise anything for Mr. Burnine," Culwell protested. "I got orders—"

"Tell Burnine to stick those orders up his ass," Shad said. "We're going to stop this thing now."

Major had never seen old Shad so aroused.

"Get started, Whitlock," Shad said. "I'll handle Burnine and my idiot sons too."

Major lived a long time going down the hill with his hands raised, calling out to Lavington. He was a hundred feet from the cabin before Lavington answered him. "All right. Come on in."

From somewhere in the cottonwoods Burnine shouted angrily, "Stay away from there, Major!"

Scared and angry, Major yelled, "Go to hell!"

He was ten feet from the door when Lavington kicked it open. Someone on the hill fired into the opening. Major heard the bullet thud into his new floor. He made a running jump of it then, flinging the doors closed as soon as he was inside.

Lavington was sighting between the logs. He could not see Jake lying prone on the hill but he saw the smoke from his shot, and he saw a man leap off a horse close to where the shot had come from.

Lavington fired the buffalo gun.

On the hill, Shad McAllister was cursing his son and striding over to kick the rifle from his hands. The heavy slug from the buffalo gun carried away part of his hip. It knocked him into a half spin and he fell across Jake's legs.

The short ride he took to Chunk's cabin, with Jake leading the horse and Culwell holding him in the saddle, was the last time Shad ever was on a horse. For the rest of his life he hobbled on the ground. In moments of bitterness he said it was his fault because he had got mad too late.

From the trees near Major's dam the Martins listened and watched and tried to piece together what was going on. From Bill Gifford they had got word that Lavington was going to be hanged for killing Tad Sherman.

It was odd that Burnine hadn't told them, Uriah thought. Gifford was not to be trusted at all. He might have been setting some kind of devilish trap for them.

Having arrived on the scene late, and by devious trails, they now figured that it must be Major Whitlock that the ranchers were after.

"You reckon they'll burn him out?" Eben asked.

"Maybe. But we ain't doing nothing, see? I don't like the smell of this whole thing." There was Gifford, with some low-down, sneak plan in his head. And there was Lafait Whitlock to worry about. He was supposed to be in Denver with Goodwin, according to Gifford.

"We're not going to do anything, understand?"

Uriah repeated. Eben was another worry. The older he got, the worse it was with him wanting to keep doing all the things that they had got away with in Missouri.

"We going to stay to see if they can burn him out?" Eben asked.

Suddenly Uriah leaned forward with a start. "Where the hell did he come from?"

Down by the finger hills near the head of the valley, a figure had appeared from nowhere, a man who moved swiftly. He crossed open ground and disappeared into the willows. "Like an Indian," Eben said.

Uriah searched out the ground with a worried frown. The man must have been hiding there all the time, for otherwise he would have had to come from one side of the valley or the other, down a hill with little cover except sparse rabbit brush and across the meadow on his belly. "I wonder if he seen us?" he mused uneasily.

"Not likely at all."

"I don't see how he could have," Uriah agreed, but still the sharp barbs of uneasiness plagued him. He wanted to leave then, but he knew Eben would argue and whine about it all the way home, being deprived of seeing a cabin go up in flames. Eben was getting more whiney all the time; more eager and careless too. Wanting those horses of Gifford's . . .

Chapter Sixteen

The gush of black powder smoke from the buffalo gun had obscured Lavington's vision after he answered Jake's shot, and so neither he nor Major knew about Shad. Major kept hoping that Shad was carrying his point against Burnine.

Heavy fire from the besiegers belied the hope. The new room, yet unpartitioned, was untenable now. Lavington was crouched at the west wall of the cabin. "What made you even think they'd give me a chance if I came out?"

"Shad McAllister promised me. I trust him."

"They're all the same. We're blind on the south, Major." Lavington's voice rose oddly, almost breaking. "They'll set us afire there."

He had a right to be scared, Major thought, but for the moment he was nearly hysterical.

"I tell you they'll get us from the south of that new room with fire!"

Major took the long rifle and went into the loft. By looking down the slant of the roof, through the gaps between the shakes, he could see the shadow-broken ground behind the new room. One shot was all he'd get, and then he'd have to drop out of the loft in a hurry.

He picked his spot and waited. If they could stave them off until dusk, the escape plan that he and Miami had cooked up might work, or maybe by that time some of Lavington's friends would show up.

He began to sweat in the stale heat close to the roof. Each shot striking the new room made him more conscious of the fact that someone might decide suddenly to send a few bullets through the loft. He could already see streaks of light where some of the shakes had been splintered. Jude would hate that.

The Pilchers, yes; you could expect them to be in a lynch mob, but he'd sort of thought that Toby and Jake McAllister were getting a little sense, especially Toby. Culwell—well, he did just what Burnine told him to do. Major wondered if old Ross Pilcher was out there. He doubted it.

He was wiping his brow to keep sweat from running into his eyes when he saw the man crawling to the edge of the trees. He couldn't see him clearly until he wormed out into the open, pushing before him a bundle of dead grass and sticks.

It was Toby McAllister. Why did it have to be him!

His companions back in the trees continued a strong fire above the crawling man. Toby rolled on his side and dug into his pocket for a match.

Major shot him in the leg.

As he scrambled down from the loft Major heard bullets snapping through the shakes.

Lavington was in the northwest corner of the cabin, reloading his rifle. "Did you do any good?" he asked.

"Slowed him down."

"I blew bark in somebody's face." Lavington was in better spirits. "Maybe we can hold out until help comes."

Jordan, for sure; O'Neal, if he happened to be around; and Lafait, though Major didn't like to admit it—he had held it in the back of his head that all of them would help him in case of something like this. "Help?" he muttered.

A bullet whipped through the thin wall of the outer room, went through the unfinished connecting doorway and smashed something on a shelf.

"Sure," Lavington said. "Polly must have gone for help after she saw all those horse tracks in my yard."

Time and distance, Major thought. She would likely go to the Stenhouse place. If Big Harve was even home, he would want to get the Groslands, maybe even the Martins. If there were not too many delays, maybe help would arrive by dusk. Maybe. Just one "if" was more than plenty.

"There's a trapdoor in the new room, Mr. Lavington. You can get out through it. After dusk Miami is going to bring a bridled horse right to the corner of the cabin."

"How can he do that?"

"He will, don't worry." Major had doubts enough about it himself, but Miami had said it could be done.

Burnine was still very much in command, but his men were through with any daylight attempt to burn the cabin. Toby was lying on the ground with a blood-soaked shirt around his leg, the calf torn and the bone in flaming agony, unbroken, but with Major's down-angling ball lodged against it.

Matt Pilcher had a shattered finger, part of the hand he had thrust around a tree to steady his rifle. One would have thought he was in mortal agony, the way he complained, until Burnine cut the few shreds of flesh holding the finger to his hand and told him it wasn't half as bad as a rope burn and to stop whining.

Ross Pilcher expressed doubts about the wisdom of staying around much longer. The Regulators might come galloping in any time.

"Let 'em come," Burnine said savagely. "We'll settle everything then, instead of having it drag on forever." He forgot his watch and looked at the sun, just setting.

He detailed Culwell and Matt to take Toby up to Chunk's cabin, and told Matt to stay there, relieving his brother Luke, who had taken Toby's place as guard after old Shad was wounded.

Dusk brought a great nervousness to Lavington. At night the flames would be much worse. He slipped around the cabin from loophole to loophole like a big cat seeking escape. "They're all around us now, Major, except on the meadow side. What happened to Polly?"

"They're on their way."

"How do you know? Maybe—"

"No if's." Major was watching through a hole at the northwest corner. "No ifs about Miami either. He'll be here."

"How's he going to get a horse in close to this cabin!" Lavington shouted.

Major didn't know that himself. "He can move like smoke. You should have seen how he fooled me when he hid in that badger hole."

Lavington moved to another loophole. "Jesus, that seems like a long time ago." He looked out into the dusk. "There's anyway two of them on the hill. Even if he gets a horse here I can't ride straight across the meadow road."

"Up the valley," Major said. "After the first hundred yards, you'll be all right."

"I won't worry if I once get started." Still looking out, Lavington asked, "What set you against Polly all of a sudden, Major?"

"Me? It was her that turned against me."

"Why?"

"I've got no idea. One day I was trying to ask her to marry me and somebody came along just then and I didn't get the job done. That's when it started, near as I can figure."

"Must be something more to it than that," Lavington said. "How was Miami going to get across the valley without being seen?"

"He said he was going to make a big circle and come down from the trees at the head of it." Because of the thicket Major could see only a short distance up the valley. He was straining so hard that his eyes saw movement where there was none. He closed them for a rest, his head pressed against the logs. Maybe Miami wasn't coming; they might have caught him and put him under guard at Chunk's cabin. Mark had bragged about how they were rounding up everyone and holding them there.

"Did you ever try asking her again?" Lavington asked.

"Who?"

"Polly!"

"Oh . . . No, I never got the chance. Bill Gifford or somebody was always around."

"You've got more brains than that, Major. You know she's been using Gifford only to make you jealous."

"I guess so." Major resumed his lookout. Jeem's cousin, it was quiet out there. All at once he had an overpowering premonition that someone had sneaked to the back of the new room. He tiptoed into the addition for a look.

Shadows were heavy in the cottonwoods. He saw no one in the trees or in the open between the thicket and the cabin, but he knew they were there, waiting, probably already creeping in with a fire bundle. He returned to the main room.

"Anything?" Lavington asked.

"Quiet." Major went back to the corner to watch for Miami.

"I've got to make a run for it."

"No! That's what they want. They'll get you sure."

"That's better than being burned!"

"Miami will be along pretty quick."

"The hell! You're going to lose this cabin, Major. They're going to burn—"

"Stop that damn yelling." Major was scared and nervous too, but he didn't see no use to beller about it.

"I didn't mean to. It's just that . . ." Lavington didn't finish his thought. He put his back to the logs. "I've got a bad feeling that I ain't going to get out of this."

Major took a quick glance at Lavington. He couldn't see the man's face very well, but his voice had a strange tone that made Major feel uneasy.

"I've got no fears about my wife and the boys, but Polly troubles me, Major. She gets hurt and tries not to show it. In some ways she's a strange girl, Major, and I don't understand her, except I know she's no ordinary woman. I guess what I'm trying to say is—"

"He's coming!" Major cried.

Luke Pilcher was closer to the meadow than any of the men in the grove. When he heard the slow thud of hoofs on sod, he swung his rifle to cover an opening in the direction of the sounds. It was just one of Major's horses, followed by the oxen that had been unharnessed and turned loose after the fire wagon dumped over.

The three animals passed the opening and went on toward Major's shed. Pets, that's what those oxen were. Sometimes they stood around in the yard like members of the family. You bet they'd high-tail fast enough when Culwell set the place on fire, which he ought to be doing just about now.

What Luke hadn't seen—far better men than he had been deceived by the trick ancient among horsemen the world over—was Miami Rusk walking on the far side of the horse, step by step with its forelegs. Luke's brothers would not have detected the ruse either, in all probability, but they were never to allow Luke to forget the fact that the thing had been accomplished while he watched from less than twenty-five feet away.

The dusk of course was a great help to Miami, who hadn't figured on the oxen at all, but they made it all the better, trailing along like that. He had his bad moments when he stopped at the corner of the cabin near a pile of scrap lumber. The oxen went on around him to the front of the building and the horse tried to follow and Miami had to haul back on the hackamore with all his strength to keep it from going.

He got the horse quieted but he was afraid that maybe he had given the whole thing away.

It wasn't long but it seemed like forever that he had to stand there, knowing that all those rifles were looking at the cabin. And then there was a rattling of dirt on boards and Lavington's head popped out of a hole behind a pile of twisted lumber scraps.

The horse tried to shy away.

It had to be done in a rush then. Lavington came out of the hole on hands and knees. He grabbed the hackamore that Miami had rubbed with black mud, leaped up bareback and turned the horse in a plunging run.

Culwell yelled, "He's coming your way, Luke!" Caught at a disadvantage while crawling toward the cabin with a fire bundle, Culwell got off one shot with his pistol, without much hope of making a hit, but more to warn everyone that Lavington was getting away.

Luke Pilcher reacted slowly to the yell. He fired after the shadowy horse and rider swept past the opening.

Lavington was away free and running. After a quarter of a mile he knew he'd made it. The glooms that had affected him in the cabin were washed away by the cool air of freedom. He'd go straight up the valley, cut over to the north mesa and then it would be an open run all the way to Pilcher Town, and damned if they would catch him before he reached the Sheplers.

In fact, they might not even try.

On one of the ridges below the aspens he stopped to let the horse blow, and to listen for sounds of pursuit. Marked against the pale eastern sky, he looked into the darkening valley and heard no sounds of running horses. It just was not worth the price, he told himself. As soon as possible he would get his family together and leave the country.

He was thinking that when Eben Martin shot him dead.

The itching hunger had been too great to resist when such a satisfying target presented itself not fifty yards away. Eben thought it was Major Whitlock, but he really did not care.

Just a fraction too late Uriah had acted after he realized what Eben was about to do. Uriah struck out with his pistol to prevent the act. The blow crashed into Eben's head with sodden impact.

He never regained consciousness. Eben was still alive when Uriah lashed him across his saddle and left in panicky haste. In the dry hills south of Kettle Drum Springs, Uriah stopped. It was about time that damn fool Eben was coming to.

Eben was dead then, but Uriah did not want to admit the fact. He rode west into the mountains and stopped on Squaw Creek at one of their hunting shelters.

Eben's body was beginning to stiffen then.

Uriah cursed him for dying so easily. Now the blame for Major Whitlock's death would be on him alone.

Darkness in the grove and lack of communication made yeasty confusion among the attackers after Lavington's escape. Burnine yelled down from the hill, asking Culwell if he was sure there had been a man on the horse. Culwell was sure enough of that, but a sudden doubt hit him: It could have been a trick to draw pursuit, and the rider might not have been Lavington at all but the same man who had brought the horse to the corner of the cabin.

Major compounded the confusion by firing all the weapons in the cabin as fast as he could, shooting aimlessly against the hill, jumping from one loophole to another.

Only Luke was sure. His look at the rider had been brief but long enough for him to identify Lavington by the way he rode; but Luke was not going to admit that he had missed a chance to shoot him.

"Everyone stay where you are!" Burnine shouted. He came down into the trees to find out for himself what had happened.

"It could have been that Miami," Culwell said.

"He could have sneaked the horse in there, then jumped on him and skinned out, figuring we'd all chase after him."

"Couldn't you tell who it was?" Burnine demanded. If they had failed again, made themselves the laughingstock of the country . . .

"I was tangled up in the brush, flat on my belly. All I could tell was that somebody got on that horse and lit out."

"Did it look like Miami Rusk to you, Luke?" Burnine asked.

"Yes. I barely saw him, just a flash, no time to aim or nothing, but now that I think of it, it did look like Miami."

"You saw that much but you didn't have time to shoot the horse from under him," Burnine said disgustedly.

"Damn it, Mr. Burnine! Back in the trees, in the dark—"

"Shut up." Burnine cocked his head, listening to the last few shots Major fired. He heard the bullets hitting high in the trees. Wild, cover-up firing. Burnine began to suspect the worst. After the last shot, he said, "Stalking horse, huh, Culwell, right past Luke and up to the cabin? You're sure you saw just one man?"

"That's all I saw." That was the truth, for the instant Lavington took the hackamore rope, Miami had dropped to the ground and started crawling toward the meadow.

Jake McAllister came stumbling through the trees. "What happened?"

"He got away," Burnine said coldly.

The long roll of a rifle shot came from the direction of the mountains.

"What was that?" Luke asked.

"A rifle shot, you idiot." Burnine was done with useless speculation. He felt his way forward to the edge of the grove and called out to Major. "I want to come in and talk."

"Come ahead. Bring your whole bushwhacking bunch with you. The door is wide open."

"He's gone." Culwell sat down on a log. He had never helped hang a man, never seen a hanging, but he had heard about them. He was glad that Lavington had got away; but he knew that if Burnine gave him orders to go after him, starting the bollixed-up fire drill all over again, he would say yes, Mr. Burnine, and follow orders.

Harry Culwell had learned that the most untroubled people of the world were those who successfully resisted thinking more than one day in either direction from the present, and not even that far if possible.

Burnine sat down at the table with a heavy sigh. He adjusted the wick of the lamp Major had just lit and stared for a moment at two long bullet gouges in the table top. Though the door was open, the odor of powder smoke still hung in the room. "We shot the hell out of your place, Major.

I didn't figure on that when we left home this morning."

Major was kneeling on the hearth, kindling a fire. He said nothing and he didn't look around.

Burnine watched him curiously. "You've listened to Goodwin too much. We need *some* law, yes, but we're not ready for the kind he's trying to set up." It irritated him when Major didn't answer. "I thought better of you once."

Relieved of tension now that his house was safe and Lavington was on his way, Major found it hard to summon anger. When the fire was going, he went over to the table and sat down across from Burnine. "You'll never be ready for any law that interferes with what you want to do, Mr. Burnine. I thought better of you once too. I ain't as cracked on law as you seem to think. To me it's just common sense that you don't hang people because you make up your mind to do it."

Burnine shook his head. "You don't seem to understand that you helped a man get away who's the cause of all this trouble. Oh, I don't say he killed Tad Sherman, but—"

"You still ain't God Almighty, Mr. Burnine."

"I never claimed to be, but I'm going to hang Brent Lavington if he stays in the country."

There was no use to argue about it, Major knew, for he and Burnine just naturally thought differently about some things. "As long as you're here, how about some coffee?"

"Make plenty." Burnine went to the door and yelled, "Come on in, boys!"

"Who says I want them in here?"

"Do you want us and the Regulators to run head-on into each other in the dark, especially now that nothing's happened?"

The new room was full of splintery holes. Jude's shakes that Major had always been so proud of were shot up. Major had shot Toby, probably busted his leg. Lavington's horse was dead in the yard. Old hatreds were worse than ever, most likely. And Burnine was saying that nothing had happened.

They filtered in from the dark, slowly, suspiciously. Before he entered, Culwell went to investigate something that puzzled him. He found his answer when he stepped into the escape hole and wrenched his knee, which was to give him trouble the rest of his life. He was the last casualty of the Deer Creek Fight.

Luke Pilcher said loudly, "Did anybody look in the loft?"

"No," Burnine said. "Why don't you do that little chore."

Luke went up the ladder until his head and shoulders were through the hole. "I can't see nothing. It's dark up here."

Burnine laughed harshly. "He can see you all right."

Luke dropped back two rungs in a hurry. Major took the lamp over to him. "Here."

"Don't be so damn smart. I didn't really figure he was there, in the first place."

Jake McAllister came out of the new room. "Who shot Toby?"

"I did," Major said.

An insane rage began to grow in Jake's eyes. "You're easy in admitting it, ain't you?"

"He could've killed him, I don't doubt," Burnine said. "Let me ask you, Jake, who fired the shot when Major was going into the cabin under a truce your father made? Who caused your father to get his hip blown away? Who was yelling at you not to shoot when you pulled the trigger? Who did all that, Jake?"

They all stared at Jake. Let *him* take the blame for their failure.

It was a bad moment, and then the wildness receded slowly from Jake's expression, and he said, "I'd better go up and see about him and Toby."

"You stay here," Burnie ordered.

"Don't tell me what to do! This whole thing was your idea, Burnine. You and your watches and your big battle plan, and that bum who was supposed to take Lavington by surprise, so no one would get hurt. You were so damn smart and sure—"

"Shut up," Culwell said. Someone was yelling urgently from the hill.

Burnine went outside. "Come on down, Matt!"

Soon afterward a horse pounded into the yard and then Matt Pilcher came running into the cabin. "The Regulators! They're coming!"

"They're late," Burnine said. "Sit down and rest yourself, Matt."

"Didn't you hear what I said, damn it? A big bunch—"

"Stop yelling your head off. Our bird has flown and we've got nothing left to fight about—tonight." Burnine sat down. "How's that coffee coming, Major?"

Chapter Seventeen

Six well armed men were strung along the edge of the south mesa. Big Harve Stenhouse figured they were late, but he had done the best he could after Polly Lavington came for help.

Jeremy York had come along, unarmed. To pray over their souls, Big Harve guessed. York had stopped at Chunk's cabin to comfort the wounded McAllisters. The erstwhile prisoners said Matt Pilcher had high-tailed it at the first noise of men riding in from the south.

Big Harve looked down suspiciously at the light streaming from Major's open doorway. "They must have got him and lit out."

Jordan squinted through the night. "It looks like several horses in the yard."

Big Harve hailed the cabin.

Burnine came outside. "It's all over. Lavington got away. Come down and see for yourself, Stenhouse."

"I don't much care for that invitation," Big Harve muttered.

Jordan said, "I'll go down."

"They've probably got a nice cross-fire trap set up."

"I doubt it." Jordan started down the hill.

"Don't get your boiler hot so quick, damn it. I'll go with you. Just hold up a minute." Big Harve shouted orders for his men to keep their places and watch the cabin, and then he and Jordan walked down the hill together.

They followed Burnine into a room bristling with silence and hostility. As soon as Jordan saw that Major was all right, he walked over to Culwell. "I owe you something, Harry."

"Whatever you care to tackle." Culwell shrugged. "No hard feelings here though."

It hung fire for an instant, and then Jordan let it pass.

"How about it, Major, did Lavington get away?" Big Harve demanded.

"Yeah. He's well on his way to the Sheplers now."

Big Harve had come set for a fight and he didn't want to back away too readily. He glared around the room and asked, "Why don't you bastards go up to the Sheplers after him?"

"You're not in a good fix to be shooting your mouth off, Stenhouse." Burnine was drinking coffee.

"He's got a point," Ross Pilcher said glumly. "Why don't we go to the Sheplers, Mr. Burnine." It was as close as he could come to reviling Burnine, but even then he cursed himself for calling him mister. He wondered why he kept riding with his sons against his will. Shad McAllister hadn't, not this time. He'd come boiling in with blood in his eye, trying to do the right thing.

Old Ross stood up. "I'm going up and see Shad."

"You'd better let my bunch know you're coming," Big Harve warned.

Ross didn't think he much gave a damn, but when he went outside into the dark, he changed his mind and yelled to the unseen men on the hill before he went into the cottonwoods to find his horse.

"The day you hang Brent Lavington is the same day you put a noose around your own neck," Big Harve told Burnine.

"You're welcome to try. You can do it up even bigger. You can walk back up that hill right now, Stenhouse, and tell your bunch to start shooting. By morning we ought to have things pretty well settled one way or the other."

Burnine's declaration by no means fitted the

thinking of everyone in the room, and that fact was quite apparent to Big Harve; but he also knew that his own men wouldn't be too eager for a senseless night fight, now that the immediate cause of their being here no longer existed. "I'd like to see a vote on that in this room."

"Go vote your own people!" Burnine snapped, nettled because Big Harve had judged the situation so accurately.

Now that he had got under Burnine's hide, Big Harve's mood changed. "Nothing is settled. What I said about the noose still goes, but it's over for tonight as far as I'm concerned."

"Over for tonight," Major said. He was looking at the little coffee mill Goodwin had given him. A bullet had smashed it. He started to throw it into the fireplace, and then he replaced it on the shelf carefully and turned to face the men in the room.

"You're a bunch of half-grown kids, and damned fools on top of that. The best man of you all is up there with a bullet in his hip, and you forced me to shoot my own brother-in-law in the leg, and you sit there and say it's over for tonight."

He lashed them with an anger that was barely under control. "Keep it up, that's all you have to do. You're going to bring land office people in here, with maybe soldiers to back them up. You're all going to lose, and who's the next one of you who's going to die?

"If you're men, you'll bring the others off the

mesa tonight, now! You'll sit here and you'll work out your fight without killing each other. . . ."

Major was still talking when Lafait and Goodwin walked in. He paused then and Goodwin said, "Don't stop, Major. We heard part of it from outside. I've got just one thing to say, the Territorial Governor is seriously considering asking the Army to send a company of cavalry in here."

"I've said about all there is." Major observed how everyone watched Lafait as he walked down the room to sit on the fireplace hearth.

Goodwin took over the task then. He was calm and persuasive. Major continued to observe the way men's eyes kept straying to Lafait.

"Maybe one side can kill the other off," Goodwin said. "Or maybe a few men with common sense will get sick and tired of it all. As Major said, keep it up and you'll have soldiers here. How are you going to like it, Burnine, with Yankee soldiers riding herd on you?"

Burnine glared and gave no answer.

Big Harve rose suddenly. "Maybe I'm one who's sick and tired of it." He stomped outside and yelled, "Come on down, boys!"

The lamp flared up and began to blacken the chimney while they were waiting. Jake McAllister turned the wick down. He looked at Major. "You could have killed Toby, couldn't you?"

"Yes."

Still armed, suspicious, the three Groslands came in, and Joe Bob Stenhouse and little Jeremy York.

"Let's see now if we can talk about the problem," Goodwin said cheerfully.

"Shall I say a brief prayer first?" York asked.

"To hell with that," Burnine growled.

For the first time since arriving Lafait spoke. He said quietly, "I think a prayer would be fine."

"Thank you." York asked for Divine guidance

Goodwin could handle it, Major thought. The room was too hot and the stink of powder smoke was still offensive. He felt enormously tired and he wanted cool air on his face.

"Before you start wrangling, I've got one more thing to tell you," Major said. He told them what he had learned about the Martins from Calf Runner.

Burnine took it calmly. "I'd already come to that conclusion. They killed Tad Sherman, too."

"You don't know that," Goodwin protested.

Major nodded at Lafait. They went outside into the cool night.

"We met Polly," Lafait said. "She was on her way to make sure her pa made it to the Sheplers."

"No reason for him not to." Major was startled when a figure came silently out of the night. "Jeem's cousin! Why don't you call out or something, Miami?"

"O'Neal's some better. Your ma says we'll move

him up here in the morning. I'll fix a travois. That is, she said, if you're all done shooting for a spell."

"You did a great job of getting that horse to the corner of the cabin, Miami," Major said.

Miami ignored the compliment. "Your ma says clean up the boar's nest a little." He started away and then he came back. "Are the Martins in there now?"

"No."

"I seen 'em just before I crept down into the meadow. They was up near the dam. That's where that last shot came from."

"O Christ!" Major hadn't heard the shot. He was struck with a terrible uneasiness. "Why didn't you say something before?"

"You go to hell!" Miami flared. "I was worried about getting back to O'Neal." He turned away into the darkness.

They were wrangling in the cabin and Goodwin was not able to contain the bitterness; but they were suddenly dead quiet after Major told them what Miami had said.

Matt Pilcher could not make it. His wounded hand was killing him, he said. All the others joined the search. First, they found the horse that Lavington had ridden. It was in the meadow with the oxen.

By the feeble light of one of Major's lanterns Jake McAllister found Lavington an hour later.

They brought him down and put him in the bullet-splintered addition to Major's cabin.

Now there was a shameful silence. If Burnine had said one wrong word, the war would have erupted in the quiet room. "Who's going to tell his wife?" he said.

"You," Big Harve growled. "You're responsible for it."

Burnine's cheeks turned white, but he held his tongue, and Goodwin broke the tension by saying, "We're all responsible. I'll tell her."

"What about the Martins?" Fred Grosland asked.

"Hang 'em," Big Harve said, and Burnine gave him a quick look as if to say, "You're stealing my thunder."

Major wondered to see it happen so easily. A few hours before they had been willing to kill each other, and now both factions were of one mind about killing someone else.

The best Goodwin could do was get them to agree that the Martins would be given a chance to be heard, and that if a majority of those present at the time voted that there was a reasonable doubt about their guilt, then they would be held for a court trial. Later, using the somewhat shaky agreement as the basis of his argument, Goodwin persuaded Major and Lafait to join the group.

Since time and distance and the immediate need of care for the wounded in Chunk's cabin were all influences against quick action that night, the mob—Major could see them as nothing else—agreed to meet at Burnine's the following afternoon, and proceed from there.

After all the others had left, Jordan and Lafait went to bed, as men who had earned a good night's rest. Major knew there was no use for him to retire. Sometime before morning, he was sure, he would have to face the part of the whole affair that he dreaded most.

Polly would not stay at the Sheplers after she knew that her father had not arrived there. At the latest, Major guessed, she would be back by daylight, and then he would have to tell her the truth.

He sat at the table, tired but wide awake, while Lafait and Jordan slept peacefully. Where had Gifford been during the shooting? No use even reflecting on it, Major thought. Maybe the man hadn't known what was coming, but even if he had known, he would have been far away on some convenient, logical duty.

He wondered if anything was really settled. Men would always find something to fight about, land, water, money, or some big-sounding principle. No matter how you tried, their trouble would some-how splash all over you.

Maybe the Regulators and Burnine's bunch were a little tired of the whole business. That talk about the Army coming in had made them mighty thoughty. There wasn't going to be any great love feast right away, Major was darned sure, but common sense might start catching on.

Two hours before daylight, Polly and Troy Shepler rode in. One look at her face and Major knew that someone had told her about her father.

She ran straight into his arms, sobbing.

"Old Ross Pilcher told us," Shepler said. "Well, I reckon I'll be getting back." He paused in the doorway and gave Major a long, hard look. "That's a mighty fine girl there, Whitlock."

They rode to hang the Martins.

It was an orderly group, determined men going openly to do what they thought was right. And it was still a mob. Burnine and Fred Grosland were in the lead. Major was riding beside Doc Kimball, whom old Ross Pilcher had searched out during the night.

Goodwin came up beside Major. "If they have any defense at all, you two are going to hold with me to see that they get a trial. Right?"

Major and Kimball nodded, and Goodwin rode on to see if he could influence some of the others.

"Where's the sheriff?" Kimball asked.

Major gave him a sour look. "Gifford. Shit."

The sod was green and the horses made no dust going toward the twin cabins. Major felt a tightness in his stomach and a dryness in his mouth. Burnine and Grosland pulled their rifles from the boots.

"Knock their horses down if they make a run for it," Burnine said.

"All their horses are in the pasture," Big Harve said suddenly. "It looks like we've got 'em, boys!"

All the horses the Martins owned were in the creek pasture. Uriah was home, but Eben was where his brother had left him at the hunting camp the night before.

Riding in at dawn on a limping horse, Uriah had rushed into his cabin and found it empty. Even before he reached the door of Eben's cabin he was shouting, "Has anyone been asking about us?"

No one answered. He ducked through the doorway and saw Alethea sitting on a three-legged stool near the fireplace.

"Who's been here asking for us?"

"Are you the doctor?"

"Stop that, you damned old fool! I want to know—" Uriah's eyes adjusted to the gloom and he had a good look at the woman. What a looney she'd turned out to be, and Fiona was no better.

"Where's Fiona?"

"Are you the doctor?"

"Goddamn it, Alethea!" She didn't know him, she really didn't, Uriah realized suddenly. She was just sitting there, vacant-eyed.

"I've got gold, doctor. We've both got gold." Alethea held out her hand with a coin in it.

Uriah snatched the coin and looked at it closely.

It was some kind of foreign junk. He put it in his pocket. "Where's Fiona?"

"She's got gold too. You'll fix our teeth, won't you, doctor?"

"Sure, I'll fix your teeth, you crazy old bat." One thing good about it, there was no problem about having to explain where Eben was. "Now where the hell is Fiona?"

"Come with me," the woman said. She had an odd sort of dignity as she walked out slowly, barefooted, her ragged dress dragging the dirt.

Fiona was hanging from a short rope in the stable.

Alethea knelt on the hard-packed floor and began to pray. Uriah stumbled out of the stable. It was his own face he had seen at the end of the rope, the neck oddly twisted and coming apart.

Ever since Eben had made his foolish mistake at Deer Valley, Uriah had known that he had to run, and now he wanted to get it done even faster.

Fast and far. Take all the horses, some food, the store of cartridges in both cabins, some blankets —that was about it. Oh, yes, the money buried in the stable. A man couldn't leave that behind.

He looked at the broken-backed shovel rusting on the ground where the women had tried to scratch out a garden. You couldn't shovel loose sand with that. He grabbed the axe from the wood-pile.

Alethea was still praying when he went inside.

Uriah jerked her to her feet. "Get me some grub together and be quick about it."

"You're running off again, Uriah."

"Oh, you know me, all right enough. All that crazy talk about the doctor—"

"Where's Eben?"

"He'll be along. Now get out of here and get that grub!" Uriah shoved her toward the door.

She staggered a few steps but she didn't leave. She stood staring at him, plucking at the front of her dress with both hands. "Did he go for the doctor?"

"Yes!" Uriah began to chop at the ground.

"You're lying to me, Uriah Martin."

"Goddamn it, get out of here!"

"I ain't going until you take Fiona down."

"All right, all right!" Uriah dropped the axe and drew his knife. He couldn't reach the rope unless he stood right against the thing hanging from it, and he was not going to do that, no matter what his hurry. She must have stood on something. . . . He saw the stool kicked over against the wall.

He was stooping to pick it up when he heard the shuffle of Alethea's bare feet close behind him. He jerked his head around and saw her face for one short moment and then the axe came down and sank into his skull.

They closed in with a rush against the cabins. No one was there. Big Harve cursed. "They've skipped!"

"There's something wrong here," Burnine said. "They wouldn't leave their horses."

Then Fred Grosland shouted urgently. "Doc, Doc, come here!"

Everyone converged on the stable. Joe Bob was leaning against the wall outside, his back humping convulsively as he vomited. Alethea was sitting on a stool, looking up at the men standing around her.

"Take her out of here," Kimball said.

Almost everyone was willing to help with that chore. At the door, someone said, "What do you want us to do with her, Doc?"

Alethea broke away from William and Ernst Grosland and ran back to Kimball. "They called you a doctor?"

"Yes."

"Are you?"

"Yes."

Alethea stared up into Kimball's bearded face like a child seeing a dream come true. But then a cruel wariness swept across her sagging features. She began to scream at him, beating her fists against his chest. "You lie! You lie! You're not a doctor!"

They took her outside by force then, and after a few moments she quit struggling and began to pray loudly. Joe Bob looked at her wanly. He had got control of himself, but the sight of the woman, swaying back and forth, with saliva dribbling from her chin, was too much for him. Another retching spasm hit him and he went stumbling toward the creek.

Big Harve watched him with a grin, and then Big Harve looked on beyond the reeling figure, at the lush meadows fed by the winding creek and flow of springs along both sides of the valley. "That grass looks better than any I've seen during this last dry spell."

They all looked, appraising the place carefully.

"That grass does look good, for a fact," Fred Grosland said carefully.

Inside the stable, Kimball batted at a swollen blowfly that came bumbling toward his face. He glanced around to see who was left. Lafait and Major. "I see that all our bloodthirsty friends have no stomach for this kind of hanging. All right, Major, I'll hold her and you cut her down."

Chapter Eighteen

A warm sun lay on Major and Lafait as they rode through the pinons on the old buffalo trail. Lafait kept yawning and complaining of lack of sleep.

"You had more sleep than I did," Major said.

"I didn't in Denver."

"Of course if you whore around all night and gamble—"

"I shoved some more money in an old boot

under your bed," Lafait said. "You seem to favor boots as a hiding place. Buy some cows or something."

A gunfighter and a gambler. Lafait just didn't look it. At the moment he was like a drowsy youngun, slumping in the saddle with his features all relaxed.

"I'm keeping track of what you've loaned me, Lafait."

Lafait grinned. "You do that, Maje, and someday when you total it all up, I'll own Deer Valley, and then I'll throw your ass out and settle down like a nabob."

They rode across Elk Creek and Major observed that the flow seemed less than the last time he had seen it.

"How long are you going to stick around, Lafait?"

"I don't know. For a while longer, I guess." Lafait fumbled with a witch's knot in the mane of his horse. The tangle proved obstinate and he gave up, yawning. "I'd sort of like to stay and see if things settle down, now that everybody can blame the Martins for everything that happened."

"Anyway, I'm glad you didn't get dragged into the fight."

Lafait grunted. "Yeah. What with you and Ma and Goodwin keeping me on the run to Denver day and night, fat chance I had to get in any of it. Not that I'm disappointed."

"Do you think the trouble will sort of fade away?"

"Seems like a good chance. Both sides have found out that they're tough. It's like two men that have mean reputations for pistol fighting. They ain't much anxious to tangle with each other."

Lafait sure should know about that, Major thought. Though he had a strong, abiding love for his brother, Major would forever have to conceal the fact that he was ashamed of Lafait's record as a killer.

Where the trail led around the hill close to Kettle Drum Springs, they looked down and saw a light spring wagon in the yard and three horses tied at the corral.

"That's Mrs. Stenhouse's rig," Lafait said. "I'll bet she brought a wagonload of women with her. When we get home, we're going to have O'Neal to nurse, because Ma will be busting to get over here to see what she can do to help Mrs. Lavington."

Major had thought he would stop by briefly to pay his respects, but one of the horses at the corral was Bill Gifford's. Gifford had been conveniently absent during the Deer Valley fight, but now he was around in all his glory, the courteous gentle-man. The sonofabitch.

Reading his brother's expression, Lafait grinned. "Don't let Gifford bother you. He ain't getting anywhere with Polly."

Major urged his horse on up the trail. "I'll ride over this evening."

Before they broke down from the buffalo trail, they could see the long sweep of the mesas with the bright greenness of Deer Valley lying between the dry flats.

A fresh surge of strength came up through Major's tiredness. There was no limit to what a man could do before he grew old in Deer Valley.

"That's a beautiful sight, Lafait!"

"Huh?" Lafait roused from dozing in the saddle.

"Just look at that!"

"Yeah," Lafait said, and went back to drowsing.

Center Point Large Print
600 Brooks Road / PO Box 1
Thorndike, ME 04986-0001 USA

(207) 568-3717

US & Canada:
1 800 929-9108
www.centerpointlargeprint.com